How To Keep Your Legs Closed In Hollywood

The Down and Dirty Survival Guide to Stardom

R.W. Mills

ORI
PUBLISHING

How to Keep Your Legs Closed in Hollywood

First Edition

ISBN: 978-0-9878343-6-2

ISBN-10: 0987834363

Published by ORI Publishing

Printed in the United States

"You fuck a movie star for over two years and he doesn't say hello or acknowledge you exist."

— Drop-dead gorgeous, aspiring actress

Warning! This book is not suitable for young children.

CONTENTS

INTRODUCTION

You are young, beautiful, and smart with a dream to make it big in the entertainment business. Can good girls survive and thrive in Hollywood, or is the casting couch the only way to go? Maybe, yes. Maybe, no. It depends on how you play the game.

Half the battle is navigating through the treacherous minefields of Hollywood, and smashing through the bewitching smoke and mirrors to see what is behind the curtain. It can be ugly back there.

Don't be daunted. When you know what you are up against, you can work it to your advantage—with your legs closed, your eyes and ears open, and your soul intact.

We all know that you've got to be in the movies or work behind the scenes.

It's your calling, your purpose, a 24-hour desire that pulses through your veins.

You are brilliant.

In one moment, you can be a kick-ass spy, and then bring the house down dressed in a period outfit while speaking in another accent.

In an instant, you can shift seamlessly between seduction, comedy and vulnerability.

You want to entertain, no you *need to* entertain millions of people around the world on a silver, or TV screen, and make a huge impact.

You want to star in movies you believe in and change the world.

You live, eat and breathe this stuff. Applause is your oxygen. The spotlight is your blood. You want to be the next Angelina, Jodi, Milla, Jennifer, Scarlett, or Grace Kelly.

In your gut, you are convinced that you will suddenly erupt onto the scene and be the next *it* girl. The go-to-girl, who will dominate the Oscars' limelight and shatter every box office record chronicled on the planet.

Young starlets get discovered all the time in Los Angeles in grocery stores like Whole Foods or while rollerblading in Venice beach, don't they?

If only it were that simple.

The truth is your journey will be riddled with daggers, obstacles, broken promises and powerful and famous dirtbags.

Sleazeballs who want to use you up, and spit you out onto the alluring streets of Rodeo Drive and Hollywood Boulevard.

Famous and powerful dirt-bags need to make room for the latest aspiring, sexy actress in town, don't you know?

So what are you going to do? Give up? No way. Sell out? Nope.

You've got to be prepared to stay one-step ahead so you won't be swallowed up alive. That's all.

This is your first Hollywood outing, and the first time you've left your small-town home, and driven 48-hours straight across the country, to Los Angeles to live the California dream.

The point is not to be taken in by the hypnotic fiction concealed by the flashbulbs on the glitzy red carpet, and most importantly, don't walk into the Hollywood shark-tank blind and get caught with your pants down.

If you're planning on re-locating to the city of angels and have saved a few thousand dollars, or if you are already there; no matter how street smart or savvy you think you might be, Hollywood is a giant sinkhole.

It's a beast with its own set of rules where anything goes. Rejection can lead to obsession. Don't become a fallen angel.

The entertainment biz apparatus was created a long time ago. It's a way of life.

What you are about to read is business as usual—Hollywood style.

This is why you need to know the juicy insider knowledge, and the outrageous survival tips to stay in one piece.

Just because you operate in good faith does not mean that they do. They don't.

You need to learn the delicious and soul-saving lessons, the dirty industry secrets, and the shocking unwritten rules the mega famous and power players know, and don't want you to know as you trek to stardom.

Besides, who isn't dying to know all the Hollywood intrigue?

While not all mega-powerful and famous men are sex-crazed, sleazy dirtbags in Hollywood, this book focuses on those who are.

Some of these enviable winners are revered around the globe, but behind the scenes, they are so twisted it surpasses rational logic.

For the sake of simplicity, the cast in this book, such as Mr. Movie Star, Mr. Big Shot, Mr. Mega Celebrity and Mr. Power Player, are virtually interchangeable.

The leading actors also cover Mr. Rock Star, other varied scumbag Hollywood power players and VIPS (very important person).

If you think playing with the big boys will get you ahead, maybe it will. Go for it, just play smart.

Don't let them play you. Learn how to play them. Work it with your head held high.

So fasten your seat-belts. We are going to take a ride through the dark side of Hollywood, and learn how to avoid the dangerous tripwires while keeping your legs closed.

Take 1. Let's get this right the first time.

Come on. Let's go.

LESSON #1: THINK YOU ARE SPECIAL?

In the real world and to people who truly care about you, you are special. You are one of God's children, but we're talking about Los Angeles here.

Not only are *you not special*. You are replaceable as fast as a New York second.

Every day there is another crop of wide-eyed aspiring actresses arriving in La-La Land with perky breasts coming to pursue their dreams of stardom for powerful and famous dirtbags to pick from, and as brutal and heartless as that might sound, you need to know that because Mr. Movie Star and Mr. Power Player know it's true.

Without a doubt, there are scads of beautiful women in all shapes and sizes in Los Angeles.

The Brazilian heartbreaker, the classic American beauty, the stunner hailing from Africa, the sultry-British import, the waif-skinny bombshell from Russia, the Scandinavian blonde hair, blue-eyed dynamo, and so on, and so on.

It's time for a reality check.

While it might be true that back home, you were a local beauty queen, and an irresistible knockout with wicked curves to die for, superficially speaking, there will always be another woman in Los Angeles who is more attractive than you are.

There will always be another wannabe actress, who is impossibly thin, compared to you, with natural, pouty full lips. Not the injected "trout pout," lips, implanted with liquid silicone you sometimes see on aging, or insecure younger starlets feeling the pressure of the camera's hot glare.

Indeed. Acting can be an impossible profession. The competition is relentless, ruthless and cut throat.

You are a small fish in a shark-infested pond among other hot, ambitious contenders seeking the same grandiose dreams of stardom, fame and fortune.

Oh, by the way, silicone belongs in cars and not in your face. Look at some celebrity before and after pictures of Melanie Griffith and Jessica Simpson to get a sense of what I mean.[i]

On the flipside, there are also women who are less attractive than you are— so hooray, hooray for you!

The point is to be grateful for your good looks, but to get over yourself, set a blow torch to your ego, and focus on what is important.

It's your God-given gifts, talents and hard work which will set you apart from the crowded playing field and not the biggest boob job ever.

There is nothing wrong with pursuing your dreams of stardom. In fact, you should, but be smart about it.

Keep your head out of Hollywood's blinding klieg lights with your feet planted on the ground.

Otherwise powerful and famous scumbags will smell ego-obsessed ambition like blood in the water—fresh blood, your blood that can turn into desperation fast. Powerful and mega-famous dirtbags will take advantage of that desperation. They will exploit it and pulverize you if you let them.

Who was that Mr. Rock Star who once so eloquently said (paraphrasing here), "Better to fuck a fatty than sleep with the same girl two nights in a row?"

Are we clear? You are not special.

In La-La Land, your commodity is in between your legs so keep them closed.

Now that's special.

LESSON #2: MR. MOVIE STAR'S LATE NIGHT CALL ROLODEX-ROTATION

If you receive a late night phone call from a dreamy Mr. Movie Star, he is not inviting you to go out for dinner, or to hang out and play monopoly.

Let's be blunt. Mr. Movie Star is calling you to come over to his place because he wants to get laid.

The only games you might play are strip poker or twister.

I know people can't take their eyes off of you, and Mr. Movie Star told you in his heartthrob, mesmerizing voice that you were something special, and he wanted to get to know every inch of you better—every inch!

But if you receive a late night phone call then you are either a part of Mr. Movie Star's Rolodex-rotation (and you need to get off), or Mr. Movie Star wants to put you on it.

What is the Rolodex-rotation? In the pre-IPhone days, a Rolodex was an alphabetized phone book organizer on cards. The cards hung on a wheel that you flipped to get a phone number.

Nowadays, it is the equivalent of an IPhone or Smartphone contact list rotation, but instead of flipping the Rolodex you scroll down or up the IPhone keypad.

This month Mr. Movie Star might be hitting the "R's" on his phone contact list. Next month he'll move on to the "Ss," and so forth. It might take a few months before Mr. Movie Star calls you again—that's the rotation part.

It's not about you unless you haven't slept with him yet, and then it is still not about you—it is about the challenge.

The Rolodex-rotation is also about variety, and adding new conquests to his favorite list of willing women who will come over and have sex with him late at night.

Remember what you have already learned. You are not special. Get over yourself. It's Los Angeles. You can be replaced in a heartbeat.

When a call from Mr. Movie Star rings on your Smartphone late at night, if you don't answer it, and let it go to voicemail, Mr. Movie Star will not go to bed alone crushed because you didn't answer his call, and he really wanted to see you, and only you.

No, Mr. Movie Star will call the next name on his Rolodex-rotation list until someone answers, goes to his place and has sex with him.

That's how *not special* you are.

Did you know there are Mr. Movie Stars and Mr. Big Shots who have sex with so many women, they include mini descriptions in their phone book next to the girls' names to help remember who is who?

Cindi Smith: Tall, no boobs, great ass, blue-eyed, redhead from Kansas. Brandi Jones: Short, blonde, big tits, killer blowjobs from Michigan.

Oh, yes. This is how these horny dirtbags operate. Still there is more to know.

A number of these men also have different phone books—one representing each city they frequently travel to or where they have more than one home (Colorado, Santa Fe, New York, San Tropez, etc.) to keep all the women they sleep with straight.

Then there are the creepy Mr. Movie Stars' who just don't care who comes over and fucks them.

They will call anyone—even women they have never met because to this cast of deviant characters, as crude as this sounds; you are a hole and a heartbeat, and the heart beat is optional.

Yessiree. Now will you get over yourself? See? Sorry, you are not special.

There is nothing glamorous about being a hole or a notch on someone's belt. *Be special* and don't go there. Now Mr. Movie Star will remember you.

Get it?

Good girls have self-respect. They would never make late night booty calls. That's all that a late night phone call from Mr. Movie Star is. Besides, who wants to be caught dead doing the walk of shame in stilettos in the morning?

So the next time your phone rings late at night, if you get weak in the knees and think you are blowing a big time opportunity with a famous celebrity or power player, you are not.

It is better to keep your legs closed and be a challenge. Mr. Movie Star might kind of learn to respect you.

Meanwhile go on with your life. In time, Mr. Movie Star might give you a daytime phone call which you can turn into a potential networking situation that leads to legitimate work based on your talent.

There are still mega-famous men out there (albeit not many), who admire women who don't take their crap, who speak their minds, are not star-struck trampy fools and work hard.

Hollywood is a business after all. It's all about making lots of money.

If a Mr. Power Player can make a profit off of you at the box office, or on the little screen, they will. Referrals from a Mr. Movie Star are helpful.

That being said, if you decide to answer Mr. Movie Star's late night call out of curiosity (let's face it, some of these conversations are hilarious, and pathetic, especially when Mr. Movie Star starts to beg... if only their fans knew), then tell him you cannot come over because you have to work in the morning despite his kind offer to send his limo driver to pick you up.

Good girls work during the day and not at night.

Good girls work vertically and not horizontally.

After you have declined Mr. Movie Star's rude, late night invite to have sex with him, expect him to grow huffy and indignant. Mr. Movie Star is not used to hearing the word "no" from anyone, especially a woman.

Mr. Movie Stars (this includes Miss Movie Stars) have become accustomed to getting everything they want.

In addition to the million dollar salaries some get paid to act, they demand a lavish lifestyle for the grace of their presence. In the coddled world of celebrity, a rider tells the tale.

A rider documents the luxurious amenities a star demands to appear at a venue or to work on a film. It could be anything and everything from softhead toothbrushes and toothpaste to private jets and adjoining rooms for their entourage at 5-star hotels.

And you—a pesky commoner, said "no," to Mr. Movie Star's invite to join him for a late night booty call? Yes, you did. Good for you.

Don't blow him, blow him off.

Next Mr. Movie Star will go all high drama and pull the Don't-you-know-who-I-am? Crap. Don't-you-know-how-busy-I-am? I-made-this-time-especially-for-you BS routine, but fuck him.

If he does not know how to treat a lady like a lady, he can take a hike.

The miserable secret some Mr. Movie Stars do not want you to know, but have confessed to women they respect (granted in a drunken stupor) is while they claim to have bedded thousands of women, they have never made love once. I repeat. Not once.

It is tragic considering there is a big difference between fucking, and making love, and they can't tell them apart anymore. Too bad for them with their money and fame they just don't get it and keep playing the late night Rolodex-rotation game, like junkies on the crack pipe chasing a high that never comes, burying themselves in empty, meaningless sex.

Ladies, get a clue.

Your life's purpose is not to be a hole or a notch on a megastar's belt. It is not to fulfill Mr. Movie Star's sexual fantasies because he lost his ability to make love because he plays the Rolodex-rotation-fuck-sport. That's their problem, not yours. Don't break a sweat.

Congratulations, you are now one step ahead of the game.

LESSON #3: HOW TO SPOT A GIRL ON THE LATE NIGHT CALL ROLODEX-ROTATION

If you meet a sweet but gullible woman, say a statuesque natural beauty with a pixie face, from a small town in Indiana, and she tells you with a starry look in her eyes that she's been having a secret affair with a Mr. Movie Star for months, take pause.

Does Miss Pixie Face trust you to tell you who Mr. Movie Star is and to keep her secret, even though you have known each other for a few days?

If so, she's probably on the late night call Rolodex-rotation.

If Miss Pixie Face, in a sing-song voice, tells you something like this:

"What [insert Mr. Movie Star's name here] loves about me is I am his special secret. Nobody knows about us. Nobody. Well, umm, except you of course," snort, giggle. "Well, what he loooves about me is I'm so discreet when I go to his place up on [redacted]; I even sneak out before the help arrives in the morning. He just loves that about me. My discretion. He completely trusts me."

Please take pity on her.

Miss Pixie Face is not the sharpest tool in the toolbox. She is on the late night call Rolodex-rotation and needs to get off that loop. Gently try to show Miss Pixie Face her misguided ways. Mr. Movie Star needs to stop using and reusing her like a Sham Wow!

I hate to rock your fantasy, but someone has got to tell the truth. If you have been sneaking into Mr. Big Celebrity's house, late at night, off and on, for months, and if he cared and respected you, he would have taken you out in public by now. At minimum, he would have taken you out in threes.

What's "threes?"

Threes work like this.

It is you; Mr. Movie Star and one of Mr. Movie Star's BFFs (best friends forever) out in public together where Mr. Movie Star's BFF pretends he is with you.

BFF is acting like a beard, by posing as your date for Mr. Movie Star. This scheme is to conceal the real relationship between you, and Mr. Movie Star, and to make the Paparazzi think you are with BFF, and *not with him*.

A BFF, acting like a beard in this way, keeps the gossip mill hushed, or guessing, and you and Mr. Movie Star can be out together without the Paparazzi hounding you.

Beards have not solely been used in Hollywood to conceal a mega celebrity's sexual orientation.

Oh, no. Get a clue and wake up.

Good girls are at the party.

They are on the movie premiere's red carpet. They are drinking mint juleps at a regal charity polo match in Santa Barbara and clinking glasses with Prince William and Kate, the Duchess of Cambridge—not tucked away, hidden in Mr. Movie Star's estate, or in some 5-star hotel suite eating room service like a late night call Rolodex-rotation girl.

LESSON #4: WHY MEGA STARS PAY FOR PROSTITUTES

W e have all read the scandal-ridden headlines. Another Mr. Movie Star or Mr. Rock Star busted with a prostitute. The shame, the worldwide humiliation, it doesn't make sense, right?

It's the same playbook every time.

Social media, like Twitter, lights up reveling in the mega celebrity's embarrassment and shame. Lewd images bounce around platform to platform. RT Haha Mr. Movie Star paid 4 that? #MrMovieStarcheapblowjob

Then *Entertainment Tonight, People Magazine, Inside Edition, New York Post, The National Enquirer, TMZ* and *The Globe* go wild tracking down the prostitute's friends.

The friends say the same thing.

Miss Prostitute is a nice girl. The story jumps across the pond, and the tabloids in the United Kingdom join in the melee.

The UK tabloids really have a knack for finding the worst possible pictures, don't they?

Next, Mr. Movie Star's mortified wife files for divorce.

Then the disgraced Mr. Movie Star goes to rehab after he publicly apologizes to his wife, family, and fans, and begs for understanding and forgiveness during this difficult time while he gets help for either a sex or drug addiction or both.

Ever wonder why celebrities, even Oscar-nominated actors, who can have non-stop sex with groupies for free pay for prostitutes and are super-johns?

Well, wonder no more.

It is because prostitutes are paid *to go away*. Prostitutes, if the price is right, also jump into the kinky, naughty sadomasochism swamp some mega-famous leading men lust over.

Good girls do not engage in sadomasochism—it's sexual activity that causes pain or humiliation. Romantic, right?

Sex with more than one woman at the same time is another reason why Mr. Movie Star calls prostitutes.

For them, having multiple women with them is like watching porn but it is live porn. Some Mr. Movie Star's cannot perform in the sack anymore (Lesson #2) so what else are they going to do? They get freaky to get off.

Prostitutes are there to get them off. The prostitutes are there to service Mr. Movie Star's wildest sexual fantasies, no matter how debauched they are. Then the prostitutes are paid to go away and keep their mouths shut—poof.

That's the scoop.

Service Announcement FYI: If you have befriended a drop dead, gorgeous would-be model, and she tells you that she sells Herbal Life or another multi-level product, but she never has any products, or order forms on her, and she's never emailed you a link to buy something either, again, take pause.

If you know that Miss Drop Dead Gorgeous is an extensive jetsetter, who has traveled all over the world, than you have met a woman who pays her bills with her legs open.

Miss Drop Dead Gorgeous Model is not selling anything that comes with a 30-day money back guarantee, or return for a full refund if you are not happy. Multi-level companies are convincing legit-job cover stories for women who are hookers.

Air-kisses anyone?

Lesson #5: Money Tight? How to Save on Rent

Is money tight and you could use a break?
A first-rate way to save money and to temporarily live rent free is by house sitting.

House sitting is where you watch and take care of another person's houses, pets and plants while they are out of town in exchange for free rent.

If you never have house-sat before, network for opportunities through friends, family or colleagues.

It's a big help to have references. If you don't have any consider asking former landlords, bosses or neighbors to vouch for your character and honesty to help get your foot in the door. House sitting durations can range from days to months.

Create a house sitting resume. Include a professional profile. No one will trust their home and worldly possessions to anyone who looks like a train wreck or coked-out party girl.

There are websites to find house sitting gigs. You can also advertise that you are available to house sit on some of them. To start, check out: craigslist.org and MindMyHouse.com (annual $20 fee).

LESSON #6: YOU KNOW YOU ARE IN A HOLLYWOOD BROTHEL-LIKE HOUSE SITTING SITUATION WHEN...

D o you think brothel-like house sitting gigs don't exist in Hollywood? Think again. They do. It's when a Mr. Big Shot provides room, and board, to a bunch of young, eye-fetching women at his mansion ostensibly out of the goodness of his heart.

Yeah right.

The only difference with this brothel is there is one client. His name is Mr. Big Shot, the mansion owner. While these Hollywood house sitting gigs aren't officially called brothels, and fly under the radar, let's keep it real and call them what they are.

You may be surprised by how many Mr. Big Shots claim they want to help women like you when you first arrive in Los Angeles by offering free accommodations at their estates.

But know this. Sure, Mr. Big Shot wants to help you, and he wants to help himself *to you* in between his bed sheets.

Don't be naïve. That adage is correct.

Nothing is free.

The Hollywood Brothel-like House Sitting Gig

If an ex-model you have befriended at a party or a yoga class, tells you about her girlfriend's house sitting gig at a mansion in Bel-Air with guest houses, and claims the owner is a nice, generous, successful man who likes to help out women; chances are high that you have encountered the Hollywood house sitting scenario.

Rent payments are expected but not in cash.

You know you have entered into a Hollywood brothel-like house sitting scenario when:

• The respective owner, Mr. Big Shot, is a very important person (VIP), like a top movie studio mogul, media elite, knock-off fashion czar, or a real estate tycoon, who develops properties like golf courses or shopping malls.

VIPS travel a lot, and they will not be around that much which is a big plus, *but they will be around sometimes. It's the sometimes you have to worry about.*

• Is the house sitting gig nestled in an affluent neighborhood like Bel-Air, the Hollywood Hills, Beverly Hills, Malibu or Marina Del Rey?

For star gazers, north of Sunset Boulevard is considered cool, south of Sunset is not.

• When you arrive at this supposedly generous man's house, is his mansion located at the end of a long private gated driveway behind electronically activated gates?

• Does the estate have sprawling manicured lawns, in lush and woody settings, with sensational amenities like tennis courts, swimming pools, Jacuzzis, screening rooms, and wine cellars?

• Or does the mansion look like a scene out of the classic 1950's film noir, *Sunset Boulevard*, frozen in the lead character Norma Desmond's time warp?

• When you meet the ex-model's friend, the woman living at the house sitting gig, we will call Madame X, is she also an ex-model, or the ex-wife of a rock star? Does Madame X have a devilish twinkle in her eyes? Has she had too much plastic surgery and Botox in a failed attempt to freeze her siren glory days on the catwalk? Her nose might be vanishing into two teeny, tiny nostrils thanks to years of snorting blow (cocaine) that her bridge collapsed because of a septal perforation (hole in the nasal septum), and she continues to require reconstructive surgery.

• Did Madame X eyeball your physique with x-ray precision either surreptitiously or blatantly when you two first met?

• Did Madame X, in a shrill, nasally voice because of her nose's septal perforation, say something like this?

"[Insert Mr. Big Shot's name here] is a very, very generous and kind man. He likes to help out new girls in town. All he asks is that you treat his belongings well and to be good to his dog. He loves that dog. He's out of town so much he hates to leave the property empty."

• Are young, dazzling woman (blondes, brunettes, redheads, from around the world), living at the mansion, and hanging out by the swimming pool, or playing tennis on the clay courts? Mr. Big Shots *help* all types of women, especially those who are chest heavy with long languorous legs.

• Did any of your potential roommates, a sassy one, who resembles a Barbie doll compliments of extensive plastic surgery, bounce up to you in a hot pink, Juicy Couture track suit, and gleefully tell you that she hooks for plastic surgery—hooks like hooker meaning she is a prostitute?

• Did that same Miss Barbie Doll lookalike recommend that if you ever get a boob job to get the biggest breast implants possible for your body frame like hers?

• Is there a young girl with raw sex appeal, and classically sculpted features rollerblading naked around the swimming pool?

If you answered "yes" to any of these questions, welcome, you have just encountered the Hollywood brothel-like house sitting gig.

The women you met pay their rent with their legs open.

While you know in your soul that something is wrong, if you find yourself in this scenario, and desperately need a temporary place to stay, below are a few steps to follow only, only if you are in a jam.

Sometimes good girls need a break too.

Remember living at a Hollywood brothel-like house sitting gig is temporary! You can play the Hollywood game if you play your cards smart.

With Mr. Big Shot's hectic travel schedule, you should be able to outrun him for a handful of months until you can find a legitimate house sitting gig or save enough money for your own place before you will be kicked out because you didn't have sex with Mr. Big Shot.

This is a predictable story board. The ending is always the same.

Bending some rules is one thing, breaking the rules is entirely another. If you do move into the Hollywood brothel-like house sitting gig, no matter what keep your legs closed.

Tell Madame X that you are from another state like Iowa, or country, and you left home for the *very* first time. This way you can act small-town naïve, and be shocked and appalled when the funny business starts with Mr. Big Shot.

Act impressed and awestruck at the magnificent house. These Hollywood house sitting gigs are at homes that are magnificent so you won't have to fake it.

Flatter, flatter, flatter.

Tell Madame X that you are a zealous animal lover. Seriously, who does not love animals?

Warning! Be careful when you are dealing with Madame X. You don't want to end up like her. She already had her chance and blew it.

Also, she is not your friend. You can bet Madame X is acting as the Madame of the house. She is filling up the spare rooms at the estate for the owner's late-night fun when he returns.

That's how she pays her rent—off of you like a pimp. Do not trust her. Stay out of her way. Know that she will play dirty. It is what it is. Madame X will not be very nice-nice to you when she discovers that you are keeping your legs closed.

FYI. Mr. Movie or Mr. TV Star, except perhaps Charlie Sheen, typically are leery about letting young women move into their mansions because an opportunist or gold digger may take photos and sell them out to the tabloids. The aforementioned VIPS don't care about that since the average tabloid reader does not know who they are. Trying to sell photos of a VIPS estate would be a waste of time.

Lesson #7: Befriend the Staff—They Could Literally Save Your Ass

Now that you have gotten the green-light to move into the Hollywood brothel-like house sitting situation, and you have moved into one of the spare bedrooms in the main house with your two suitcases and laptop, what should you do after you have unpacked?

Immediately befriend the employees living or working on the premises.

It could be a pool-guy, butler, housekeeper, or a personal assistant.

Mr. Big Shot's staff could become your best allies ever. These great men and women, who for the most part are overworked, and underappreciated, can tip you off to Mr. Big Shot's ETA (estimated time of arrival) and travel schedule.

This is important information for you to know so you can be conveniently out when he comes home.

Even better, you could be spending a few days in the desert with friends in Palm Springs.

If you are not at the estate when Mr. Big Shot comes home, he can't make any sexual advances to collect his rent.

His staff can save your ass—literally. Just so you know— they are disgusted, and less than thrilled by his despicable dirty old man behavior too.

Sharpen up, ladies. Be smart. Plan ahead.

Buy some time. You can do it. His staff will help.

LESSON #8: NEVER DATE THE SEXY POOL BOY OR HOT YOUNG NEPHEW

Although Mr. Big Shot may employ a struggling sexy MIMBO (male bimbo), at the Hollywood brothel-like house sitting gig, who kind of reminds you of Enrique Iglesias, to clean the pool, and run errands, the MIMBO is completely off limits to you.

This rule applies to any of his cute relatives, like a super hot nephew, who is staying for a few months to learn the family business.

All guys at the Hollywood brothel-like house sitting gig are off limits to you.

MIMBOs or hot relatives are not yours to flirt with or play with. If you do break this cardinal rule, it is guaranteed that one day very soon you will arrive at the mansion to find your belonging packed up and dumped haphazardly on the private driveway.

It will be the MIMBO who is ordered to pack up your stuff.

Have some class.

Don't play where you live. End of discussion.

Lesson #9: Meeting Mr. Big Shot for the First Time

The first time you meet Mr. Big Shot, who reminds you of a 100-year old, malevolent garden gnome; it could be a few weeks after you first moved into the Hollywood brothel-like house sitting gig since he has been out of town on business.

Lucky you, but now the day of reckoning has arrived.

When Mr. Big Shot comes home, he will most likely have another fresh-faced actress goddess on his arm. If this is the case, it is very good news for you.

Mr. Big Shots can't help themselves. They need to be seen with a hot babe at all times. Obviously this latest goddess is another one of the young women he is helping out of the goodness of his heart—Hollywood style.

Who is she? She could be the girl who he lent one of his cars to use while he was out of town. If that's the case, the young goddess will be the one waiting for him at the airport to pick him up to take him home. *Oh, so that's where his Mercedes convertible has been all this time—with her.*

Warmly greet him and the young goddess.

Act jubilant to meet her because *you are jubilant* she is with him because that means he is not making a move on you— yet. There is no acting required. Then start exchanging some pleasantries and a small talk monologue using basic stroke-the-ego comments like:

"Welcome home [insert Mr. Big Shot's name here]! It's so nice to finally meet you. I've heard so much about you. It's an honor to meet you. Thank you for letting me stay in your magnificent home. It's so unbelievably generous of you. I don't know what to say. I am speechless. I can't thank you enough. This is my first time in Los Angeles, and it is overwhelming.

I feel like a fish out of water. I've read/seen/looked up [insert something about Mr. Big Shot's mammoth accomplishments here]. I can't believe I'm living here as your guest! It's a dream come true. Thank you. Thank you! Thank you for your amazing kindness."

Followed by comments directed specifically *at them* like:

"*You two* make such a lovely couple. I'm so glad to meet you [insert young goddess' name here]. I hope one day to find a relationship like *you two* have ... You look so happy together. *You two* give me hope that one day I'll find the happiness *you two* have."

Make sure that you really lay that last part on thick, repeating "you two," and "couple," as often as possible because this enforces to Mr. Big Shot that you truly believe that he is a couple with the young goddess, and more importantly that you and Mr. Big Shot are not.

So when the young goddess leaves the following morning, and he eventually makes a move on you, you can act appalled at his shocking suggestion to have sex with him, and say things like this:

"What! Me? But you and [insert young goddess' name here] looked so happy. You are a couple! I could never do that to another woman. I remember when my uncle cheated on my aunt and how devastated she was. It took my aunt years to get over his betrayal. It was never the same again... But, but, but, but... you and me? I thought, I thought... You and [insert young goddess' name here] are such a beautiful couple. You two looked so happy together. I don't know what to say. I thought..."

You get the picture, right?

After your exquisite acting routine, Mr. Big Shot will briefly be shamed. He will slither back to his wing of the house, buying you some more time until he plots when to make another play for you to collect his rent.

Bravo!

You get a standing ovation here, but remember you are only as good as your last act.

Don't let the applause go to your head. You have little time to pat yourself on the back. Mr. Big Shot will return for an encore performance.

LESSON #10: OMG WTF! OMG WTF! OMG WTF!

When Mr. Big Shot is back in town following is a quick tip to help you buy more time to outrun his sexual advances if you are also at the mansion, and were unable to get out of town (Lesson #7).

If you hear a car pull up, look out the window to see who it is. If another young budding starlet has arrived to visit Mr. Big Shot, promptly call him to see what he is doing because you thought it might be nice to hang out when you damn well know he is busy.

This gesture will temporarily ingratiate you to him.

But be very careful and stay on the alert. You must heed this warning.

It is all fun and games until it isn't. It is not beneath Mr. Big Shot to try and sneak into your bedroom while you are sleeping.

That's right, heed this warning. If there is a lock on the door, lock it before you go to bed. If not, put something in front of the bedroom door like a chair or suitcase that will fall over, and wake you up, if he opens your door.

You might find yourself sleeping with one eye open.

Mr. Big Shot probably won't try anything with you right away (remember he was with the young goddess the first evening he was home), but don't be surprised if you hear him tiptoeing into one of your stunning roommates' bedrooms late at night to collect his rent.

If that's not spine-chilling enough, the prognosis could get worse. When you hear Mr. Big Shot is opening one of your roommate's creaky doors, hopefully you won't hear him say in a loud whisper to her something hair-raising like, "Daddy is here. Come to daddy."

If so, it is freak out time. *OMG WTF! OMG WTF! OMG WTF! OMG WTF! NOOOOOOOOOO!!! I need to un-hear that immediately. Someone bleach me.*

Makes you want to take a shower, right? No, you are not dreaming. Welcome to the smarmy side of living-large in Los Angeles.

Still envy the bimbo with the billionaire, and some of the garbage you watch on what some folks call Reality TV?

"Daddy is here. Come to daddy."

If he pulls that nasty crap on one of your sexy roommates, know this. It is only a matter of time until he will be knocking on your door and saying, "Come to daddy," to you.

Visualize the huge downside of living in a Mr. Big Shot's fabulous mansion. Can you imagine, a guy who reminds you of the character from the *HBO* series, *Tales from the Crypt,* knocking on your door, saying, "Daddy is here. Come to daddy," and coming closer?

He will. That's how they roll.

Bummer.

You don't need a six sense to know that your temporary Hollywood brothel-like house sitting gig will go downhill from there. Plus it will be hard for you to look at Mr. Big Shot in the same way again despite the illusion of respectability he presents to the world—you know better.

"Daddy is here. Come to daddy."

Eww, cringe-worthy, distressing.

Don't panic just yet.

Find out when he is leaving town again and when he is coming back (Lesson #7).

Start preparing your exit, and learn Lessons #11 and #12 to buy you more time while keeping this scoundrel at bay.

The clock has started ticking now.

You can still squeeze out more time, but your days living at the mansion are numbered for the gross-out factor alone.

LESSON #11: HOW TO OUTRUN A DIRTY OLD MAN'S SEXUAL ADVANCES TO BUY TIME

Sexual harassment is sexual harassment.

It is a disturbing phenomenon that happens everywhere, but especially in the dark, warped side of Hollywood.

Keep your legs closed, eyes and ears open, and learn how to outrun unwanted sexual advances.

A good overall rule to live by is to do no harm, but take no shit.

If you discover that Mr. Big Shot is planning an extended stay, say like two weeks or so, you could inevitably find yourself in an uncomfortable jam. So let's make it as comfortable as possible.

There are a couple easy things you can do to buy more time to outrun his sexual advances. Clearly, these are temporary fixes.

Option 1: Leave the estate early in the morning, but before you go, make sure people at the mansion, preferably staff or other bombshell roommates, see you leaving looking horrible.

Smudge some black makeup under your eyes. Add a pale, gaunt hue to your face. It helps to stay up late the night before to look exhausted because you are exhausted to ensure the she-looked-like-crap act is authentic as possible.

Pretend to go to the hospital but go to the drug store instead and buy Monistat 7 to treat a yeast infection.

Do not, I repeat, do not buy the Monistat one-day dose, buy the seven-day dose. The Monistat seven-day dose gets you seven more days to bypass any sexual moves Mr. Big Shot might be planning.

Don't go directly back to the mansion after your drug store run. Kill some time. Grab some breakfast or a sweet kale, banana and strawberry smoothie or fruit-infused elixir somewhere.

Do something, anything, so you can tell Mr. Big Shot that you were waiting at the emergency room to see a doctor who diagnosed you with a very nasty yeast infection. *Must be the stress living in a new town and being homesick ...* Make sure he sees the Monistat 7 package.

You want to be an actress, right? Well, your acting skills will come in handy once again. Presto! You have just bought yourself a sexual-harassment-free-week at the Hollywood brothel-like house sitting gig.

Below are some handy facts about yeast infections excerpted from Womenshealth.gov.

Read it because it will help you know what to say as you are describing your fake yeast infection symptoms to Mr. Big Shot and your dazzling roommates when you get back to the estate.

Yeast infections are common. Some of your voluptuous roommates probably have had them.

Most men get queasy when they hear about women problems so your exchange with Mr. Big Shot should be brief. Men are babies that way. You can find plenty of additional details on yeast infections at other medical websites. Note what is in bold.

"The most common symptom of a yeast infection is extreme itchiness in and around the vagina. Other symptoms include:

• Burning, redness, and swelling of the vagina and the vulva

• Pain when passing urine

• Pain during sex

• Soreness

• A thick, white vaginal discharge that looks like cottage cheese and does not have a bad smell

• A rash on the vagina

There are many things that can increase a person's risk of getting a vaginal yeast infection, such as: stress, lack of sleep, illness, poor eating habits, including eating extreme amounts of sugary foods, pregnancy, having your period, taking certain medicines, including birth control pills, antibiotics, and steroids, diseases such as poorly controlled diabetes and HIV/AIDS, and hormonal changes during your periods"

Hopefully, Mr. Big Shot will be leaving town again in seven days. If not...

Option 2: Go to the nearest hospital emergency room. You are not pretending this time. You are actually going to go to the hospital. When you finally see a doctor, tell the doctor that you are on vacation from another city, state, or country.

Tell the doctor that you do not have any health insurance, but you know that you are suffering from a bladder infection (also known as a urinary tract infection) because you have had them before.

Since you are on vacation, your funds are limited, and you want to keep the costs down.

Ask the good doctor if he/she would please, pretty please, give you a prescription to tie you over for a couple weeks until you can get home to see your family doctor.

To describe a believable bladder infection, one of the symptoms you need to say that you are suffering from is whenever you go to the bathroom you feel a stabbing or burning pain. You must also tell the doctor that you are suffering from pain in the pelvic region when you are not peeing, and your lower back hurts.

Make sure you include those last points otherwise the doctor might write you up a prescription for a minor bladder infection—that means antibiotics for a handful of days.

A prescription for a handful of days is not good enough. Mr. Big Shot is in town. He has been trying to get physical with you and to cop a feel.

You need a longer, more powerful dose of antibiotics to buy you more time to outrun him—at least 10-14 days. That's the length of time you are supposed to take the antibiotics to treat the bladder infection.

Next, emphatically promise the doctor that once you return home you will go and see your family doctor to double check that it really was just a bladder infection and you should be good to go.

But, and this is a big but, before the doctor finishes writing you up a prescription, be sure to ask when you can have sex again because right now it is too painful with this terrible bladder infection.

Do you want to be an actress? Yes?

Here's another chance to shine.

If your acting skills are good, you might be able to steer the doctor to write on the medical prescription itself: NO SEX UNTIL IT IS CLEARED.

If so... applause! You got the money shot.

You bought yourself a couple weeks to dodge Mr. Big Shot's sexual advances at the mansion.

For more information on urinary tract infections, and in your case a fake bladder infection, you can always check medical websites to learn about the different antibiotics most commonly prescribed to treat them and other symptoms.

By the time you arrive back at the estate, Mr. Big Shot will have heard about your emergency room visit. He will want to know what happened and if you are okay.

This will be a great moment when you can show him your prescription which should say, "NO SEX UNTIL IT IS CLEARED."

After your fake bladder infection performance, make sure you reiterate how awful you feel and thank him for his concern.

You have just bought yourself a couple more sexual harassment free weeks at the Hollywood brothel-like house sitting gig.

Applause.

Kudos to you.

LESSON #12: HOW TO MAKE YOURSELF USEFUL—NOT IN THE BEDROOM

You are not staying at Mr. Big Shot's marvelous mansion to be a freeloading prima donna, lounging around the swimming pool all day, eating bonbons, tweeting, taking selfies, and uploading them onto Facebook or Instagram to show your friends back home.

You are on a mission to achieve your Hollywood dreams of stardom, working and saving some money. Take 2.

When a Mr. Power Player thinks he sort of needs you, he will turn down or off the sexual advances, and leave you alone for a while.

Remember that you are still replaceable so don't get too cocky or comfortable.

By showing Mr. Big Shot it is handy to have you around for multi-faceted reasons *other than sex* may buy you some more time at his fabulous estate.

It can also increase your living arrangement longevity and quality of life.

Looking over your shoulder to see if he is sneaking around to make another play for you to get his rent can wear you down and stress you out. It sucks.

So make yourself useful and as indispensable as possible for as long as you can. How? It's easy.

Most Mr. Big Shots have offices at home and the studio, etc. All big time actors do. This is an excellent place where you can be useful and pay your rent with your legs closed.

For starters, take an interest in his business. Learn. Watch. Listen. Ask questions, lots of questions. Everyone loves to talk about themselves. Pitch in around the office whenever you can since you should already have a job and be working, right?

While you would rather be writing an Oscar acceptance speech and deciding on which dress to wear on the red carpet all that will have to wait until your ship comes in.

Until then, it is not beneath you to answer the phones if Mr. Big Shot's assistant is sick or needs back-up. You can also help run errands whenever you can.

Mega-power players typically have business interests around the country and worldwide—New York, Europe, Japan, Singapore, all over the place. So conducting business matters in different time zones will apply. You can help out when you are not working at your other day time job.

If Mr. Big Shot is working on different projects, see if there is one you can get involved with.

Be humble, eager to learn and show initiative. Don't be lackadaisical or irresponsible with Mr. Big Shot's business or act like doing odd jobs is beneath you.

Mr. Big Shot isn't a powerful mega-bucks success because he's an idiot. He might be a dirty old man, but that doesn't make him twisted or dim-witted in other areas. You might learn something.

Countless A-listers worked less than glamorous jobs until their pot of gold of fame and fortune came along. Unless you were born in the right cradle, and nepotism applies, you can't escape not paying your dues.

Don't despair; the struggle makes any success you have that much sweeter.

Reportedly, Brad Pitt worked as a chicken mascot handing out flyers for a fast food restaurant, and as a limo driver for strippers headed to bachelor parties before his break big.

Eva Mendes sold hot dogs at a mall. Ellen DeGeneres shucked oysters in Louisiana.

Johnny Depp sold pens. Some mega celebrities used to deliver pizzas while others worked as waitresses, busboys or bartenders.

If you have a college degree or university diploma, nobody gives a damn whether or not you went to school.

It's Los Angeles. It's about what you have accomplished recently and what you can do for someone next. So get over yourself, and any pieces of paper with shiny seals that have your name on them.

Learn some new skills that will set you apart from your bedazzling roommates, who pay their rent with their legs open.

If your Mr. Big Shot is in the entertainment business, offer to read scripts. After all, you are the marketplace who he wants to attract to buy tickets to watch his films. Your opinion matters. Give him honest opinions. Reverence brings underwhelming results.

Ask if you can join in to watch dailies (in short dailies, also known as rushes, are rough cuts of footage shot at the film set that directors and other movie crew watch to review to see if any re-shoots need to be taken) in the screening room.

By watching dailies, you will learn about how movies are made, special effects, all kinds of things.

Once again, offer Mr. Big Shot your honest marketplace opinion. A lot of folks are intimidated by powerful people and "yes" them instead of providing constructive criticism that everybody needs.

Living at his estate could be an excellent place to learn about the movie biz.
Why not seize the opportunity and make the most of it for as long as you can?

If Mr. Big Shot is a land developer, you can start to learn about architecture, budgets, development permits, scaled site plans, dealing with zoning offices, and much more by helping out and pitching in.

You never know who you might meet through Mr. Big Shot either that could lead to a recommendation for a dream job in the future.

If Mr. Big Shot is a fashion designer, you can learn about fabrics, design sketches, styles, fashion trends, marketing, planning fashion shows, modeling and so on. Do you catch my drift?

Does he have kids?

If the answer is yes, this is another area where you can pitch in to pay your rent with your legs closed. While his children probably have nannies and might only be at the mansion on weekends (typically Mr. Big Shots are divorced), you can still spend time with them when they are visiting.

Depending on their ages, you can get involved in different ways. Birthday parties, or play dates, baking cupcakes, swimming lessons, sports, homework, outings, just show genuine interest in his kids. They need it. Please no acting skills here.

Kids of the rich and powerful might have everything materialistically speaking, but many of them are deprived of true affection from their super fabulous famous or powerful parents.

Further, it is harder for Mr. Big Shot to dump you onto the street when you won't have sex with him if his kids like you.

It is also tougher to get rid of you if you are handy in other areas like his business and his business associates respect you. That being said, remember do not get too comfy at the mansion because eventually he will throw you out.

Meanwhile, Madame X has her nose in everything. She is not pleased with you ever since Mr. Big Shot told her that you keep your legs closed.

As part of their conspiratorial, quid pro quo relationship, she is already on the hunt for your replacement to add to her stable of girls at the mansion.

That day will come when Mr. Big Shot's staff will be ordered to pack up your things and dump them on the driveway.

This is to make room for the new girl with a sultry face, and legs that go on forever, that Madame X has found as your replacement—who understands the insider rules and how rent is collected. They always do. Madame X needs to pay her rent too.

That's how they roll.

Until that time comes, by helping out Mr. Big Shot in different ways, you are paying the rent for one, two, three, maybe four months (five is pushing it)—with your legs closed and your head held high.

LESSON #13: NEED WHEELS AND CAN'T AFFORD A CAR? HOW TO GET THE USE OF A CAR OR LIMO

G etting around Los Angeles is not easy without wheels. You have to drive at least 20 minutes to get anywhere.

While public transportation exists in parts of Los Angeles, it is inadequate. It does not reach any private estates on exclusive Bel-Air roads or go up windy, narrow streets in the Hollywood Hills, or pass by a villa perched atop of a hill in the Pacific Palisades or Malibu.

You need your own transportation.

While you have been carpooling and imposing on friends to help get you around, here's how you can get the temporary use of wheels from Mr. Big Shot if you play your cards right.

All you need is a little help from a friend with a car or a pick-up truck. It has got to be someone who Mr. Big Shot, Madame X or anyone else at the mansion has not seen you with before.

Ask your friend to drop you off at Mr. Big Shot's mansion when he is in town late one night; say around 11:00 p.m.

When Mr. Big Shot or one of his staff, (and that includes Madame X) sees you, they will tell Mr. Big Shot that you were dropped off in a strange vehicle.

The next morning he will ask you who that was.

When that happens, this is when it is time to switch on your acting talents again.

Roll your eyes, be sure to include dramatic pauses in your delivery, and say something like this,

"Oh, him. I don't know his name. I was hitchhiking. He picked me up and gave me a ride. I got lucky. He was a life saver. He could have been a real nut case. I hate hitchhiking, but I didn't have enough money to call a cab, and I had to work late. I hope I will be able to save up enough money soon to buy a car."

Most likely Mr. Big Shot will freak out when he hears that you have been (fake) hitchhiking. He might fly into his knight in shining armor mode and say something like,

"As long as you live under my roof, I'm responsible for you. You cannot ever hitchhike again."

Bingo. That's exactly what you want to hear.

God forbid you were hitchhiking and something terrible happened to you—that could mean bad press for him.

Next Mr. Big Shot will probably give you the use of one of his extra cars, like the black Jeep or red Mazda Miatas parked in the eight-car garage on his estate.

He might give you access to his limo driver to use sometimes.

If he gives you access to his chauffeur, and you have never been in a limousine (not the tinted window Towne car, but a stretch limousine), there is only one thing you need to know that you should never do.

Do not take Mr. Big Shot's stretch limo through a fast food drive-thru like at a McDonalds.

Why? The limo will get stuck. It fits in the lane to place your order, but it cannot make the bend through the driveway to reach the food counter to pick up your food. Oopsie.

Not only will you toss the McDonald's staff into a frenzy trying to help guide the chauffeur out of the driveway without scratching the limo, you will piss off all the drivers behind you.

If Mr. Big Shot finds out, he will be furious.

LESSON #14: NEED EXTRA CASH? HOW TO GET SOME GREEN

Good girls are not gold diggers. They are not going to sell their souls for shiny trinkets and pretty baubles no one can take with them when they die, but good girls are not stupid either and like nice things.

Good girls accept all donations.

A donation is a donation. You are not obligated to do anything if someone wants to help you out. Everybody has struggled at one time or another in their lives, so don't let your pride get in the way if someone sincerely wants to give you something or help you out. Take it and say thank you.

If someone is in a position to give and lift up another person, they should. To give makes the givers feel good too. It is a blessing. Giving from the heart is beautiful, but if anyone gives you something, and tries to hold it over your head, it becomes a curse.

Anyone who does that is an asshole. There is no reason why you should speak to that person again.

Trophy Girlfriends

Let's look for a moment at trophy girlfriends who are "kept" by wealthy men. Kept women are sometimes referred to as glorified whores. A Miss Trophy Girlfriend is the perfectly coiffed, and manicured, younger woman who is with the incredibly wealthy, doddering, fossil-like man—think *Playboy's* Hugh Hefner.

Miss Trophy Girlfriend lives on a tight leash and pays a big price for the lavish lifestyle Mr. Sugar Daddy provides.

Is that her boyfriend or great-grandfather?

Ladies, there is an unspoken motto among Mr. Sugar Daddies regarding women they keep that they do not want you to know about.

Keep them broke, and it keeps them around.

Translation? Mr. Sugar Daddy gives his bejeweled Miss Trophy Girlfriend enough money to get her hooked, and dependent on the ultra-high-maintenance lifestyle, but not too much money so she can leave if she's not happy, and be self-sufficient.

It's like feeding a drug addiction, but this is a stuff addiction.

Miss Trophy Girlfriend's have monthly allowances, lots of shiny trinkets, baubles and perks, like spa days, accounts at various shops and restaurants, credit cards (with limits) and travel opportunities, but in exchange they pay the price.

Having sold their soul into splendid bondage, these women lose their independence and live at the mercy of another person—the much older Mr. Sugar Daddy.

His wish is her command.

Whenever he yanks her leash, summoning her to join him, watch how fast she stops whatever she is doing and jumps.

In the middle of lunch at the Ivy and eating the fresh Santa Barbara crab salad with some friends? One call or text from Mr. Sugar Daddy (or his executive assistant), and Miss Trophy Girlfriend will drop her fork mid-bite, and leave her friends behind at the Ivy in the dust.

The same applies to satisfying all of his sexual whims. Jump. How high?

Talk about cramping your style.

Ladies have some self-respect. You are not a dog.

Point taken?

Okay, let's go back to the original lesson.

If you could use a little extra spending money, there is one rule that applies. All Mr. Big Shots' will give you extra money in front of another woman.

Why? Because this is his way of using you to impress the latest, luscious damsel de jour, who caught his eye at a party that he wants to screw.

If you are short on cash, let Mr. Big Shot know that you are broke in front of another damsel. Ask him nicely if he can help you out.

He will because Mr. Big Shot's love to pull out of their pocket a thick wad of $100 bills secured in a Gucci engraved monogram money clip in front of another damsel. They do not want the next woman they are trying to have sex with to think they are a cheapskate. Next they will peel off a few crisp Ben Franklins and hand them to you in front of her.

The damsel in turn will see this and hope that if she plays her cards right, one day she may be on the receiving end of his generous money clip like you.

Well done.

You just got your hands on some extra cash. Not bad, huh?

LESSON #15: EAT LIKE A QUEEN—HOW TO NEVER GO GROCERY SHOPPING AGAIN

Money is tight. You are saving for a car, but a girl has got to eat. So why buy groceries when you can eat out?

Be practical, ladies. Who does not like being wined and dined? If men are asking you out for lunch or dinner, go. Take home a doggie bag, enjoy and have fun.

Up for a mouthwatering meal at Providence, Thai food at Night + Market, casual Chinese chicken salad at one the café's on the Sunset Strip, Italian at Mozza, or Mr. Chow's in Beverly Hills? Sound good?

There are scores of delectable restaurants in LA to choose from with a wide range of cultural diversity.

Restaurants like Scarpetta, The Polo Lounge, PUMP Lounge, and Wolfgang Puck's Spago, are not only lip smacking but celebrity hangouts too.

It's good to go out and network.

A big part of winning the Hollywood game is not what you know, but who you know.

Restaurant Ordering Tips to Keep you out of Grocery Stores

While carbohydrates are practically considered to be illegal in California, this is about saving money, reducing, if not eliminating, the need to go grocery shopping and your survival.

So when you eat out order an appetizer and an entrée. Who doesn't like a hearty clam chowder, calamari, grilled Portobello mushrooms, spring rolls, or Carpaccio?

Eat the appetizer and the bread from the bread basket to fill you up. After taking a couple bites from your entrée, tell your dining companion you are full and hate to waste. Ask for a doggie bag, and you have your next meal. See how that works?

Since you will be getting carbohydrates from the bread basket, avoid ordering pastas or risottos dishes for your main course.

Salads get soggy in doggie bags so order the salad dressing on the side. Be sure to order plenty of protein for your entrée like meat, chicken or seafood.

Vegans should load up on Pad Thai without egg, and shrimp, veggie burgers, couscous, falafel, tabbouleh or any stir-fried vegetable dishes.

Fruit salads and cocktails with freshly squeezed fruit juices will ensure you have covered all the food groups and ingested plenty of vitamins like C.

Even if you are a struggling actress, flat-broke, and living in a tiny studio apartment in Hollywood, or sharing a house with eight other people off of La Brea.

If you order wisely when you are dining out, you can eat like a queen every day.

More How to Avoid Grocery Store Tips

Go to any all-you-can-eat buffet restaurants. You can Google "all you can eat in Los Angeles" to find out which ones are near you. While you are online, keep your eyes open for groupon restaurant deals too.

Bring a plastic Tupperware container in your big Chanel knock-off purse, and slip in some extra food when no one's looking. Your $12.99 lunch bill can feed you all week.

Happy-hour at upscale hotels like the Beverly Wilshire can be a life saver in a pinch if you are famished and broke.

Crashing film sets is another nifty tip if your tummy is growling to keep you out of grocery stores. You can spot them all over Los Angeles.

Movie and TV film sets have plentiful catering available for the cast and crew. Join them.

If you are busted for crashing, usually people find you amusing. Even better, crashing a film set has the dual purpose of not only eating but networking.

If you play your cards right, you might end up being in the movie.

Bon Appetite!

LESSON #16: SEX, SMACK, BLOW, CRANK, X, CLOUD NINE, OH MY!

Fade in. The facts and statistics about drug and alcohol abuse in Los Angeles country paint a grim picture.

According to the American Psychological Association, in 2014, "it is estimated that the economic cost of alcohol and drug abuse is more than $240 billion annually... About $97 billion is due to drug abuse."[ii]

Drug use and abuse is a problem whether you are rich, or poor, no matter where you live.

Hate to generalize but in Los Angeles there are groups of Mr. Big Shot *drug users* and *drug pushers* for which stereotypes apply and are usually spot-on.

Case in point: the drug addict. Some Mr. Big Shots use different drugs all day long.

They use drugs to wake up, drugs to keep them up, and even more drugs to catapult an already wasted Mr. Big Shot even higher, followed by the beddy-bye, knock-out drugs. With this screwed-up bunch, there is always some substance running through their veins.

Drugs remove inhibitions.

People who are high do things they would never do if they were straight. Take this route and you are cooked.

This is especially applicable in the sex realm.

For a drug addict, drug use plays a role, but does not excuse any of Mr. Big Shot's depraved sexual predilections that are sickening. Look out. It's a freaky world out there.

These sexual acts can involve defecating and golden showers that for reasons unknown supposedly get these guys sexually off through humiliation, and helps to bring them to orgasm. Let's be blunt. Shitting and peeing belongs in toilets and not on/in wasted people.

Then there is the deadly choking game. The choking game, also known as auto-erotic asphyxiation, is the "method of increasing sexual excitement (orgasm) by restricting the oxygen supply to the brain, usually by tightening a noose around the neck," and other assorted nastiness. [iii]

What used to be taboo is becoming main-stream. It is being re-packaged as acceptable pop culture and experimental sex.

These drug heightened sex activities are so much fun; they ruin lives. The facts don't lie. Grotesque sex acts have caused, and continue to cause drug addictions, serious illness, infections, suicidal thoughts and premature deaths.

Getting high with a perverted Mr. Big Shot sounds like glorious fun now, right?

Ask the *Kill Bill* movie star, David Carradine, how much fun the choking game was—oh, you can't. That's right. He was reportedly found dead hanging with a rope tied around his neck and genitals playing the choking game.[iv]

The next stereotype is the reformed drug addict crowd. These are the Mr. Mega Stars who go to Alcoholic Anonymous. They don't drink or do drugs anymore, but they like to watch other people get whacked-out on drugs in a weird, hypnotic trance. It's as though they think they can catch a residual effect of getting high from the person who is wasted.

Lastly, meet the dangerous Mr. Big Shot drug pushers, who aren't drug dealers per se.

This cabal doesn't touch drugs themselves, but encourages women to get high and offer to provide them with drugs.

They might be a sharp-witted, clever, and a charismatic gang, but the reason they do this is because they want to control you. By giving you drugs, they are putting you at their mercy, like a straitjacket, by needing another hit/fix/line eventually.

This way they can get you to obediently do sexual deviant things you normally would not do if you were straight. It's the vicious drug trap.

What better way to take advantage of a young aspiring actress then by getting her fucked up?

These men exploit, objectify and abuse women. You are not a human being to them, but something to use.

Day in and day out, these Mr. Power Players and Mr. Movie Stars contribute to the delinquency of minors.

Do you believe that any of them who are pushing drugs on good-looking, young girls are asking to see a government issued photo id first? It's frightening when you realize that some of these power players are the world's winners. Oh, to be a fly on the wall.

Mr. Power Players who don't touch drugs, but push them on young women also pass women among each other—pimping them out for their sexual satisfaction. Nothing is off limits with this gang of deviants. They are cold-blooded psychopaths with no conscience. Run and don't look back.

Finally, there are the pill pushers. Have you met a Mr. Power Player or Mr. Movie Star who has a chest of drawers, overflowing with orange prescription bottles for pain pills or muscle relaxers like Valium, Oxycotin, Ambien, Soma, Percocet, Vicodin and Xanax, who hands them out as party favors?

If you mix pills with booze, even with bubbly in champagne flutes brimming with Veuve Cliquot, Dom Perignon or Cristal, your judgment will be impaired in no time making you easy prey for sexual exploitation.

It is important that you know the drug lingo. This way if you meet a Mr. Mega Celebrity, and he offers you drugs, because he claims that he wants you to be happy (which is total BS), you know what he is talking about.

- Blow = cocaine/crack
- Ecstasy, X, Skittles, Cloud Nine, Happy Pill = MDMA   a dangerous psychedelic amphetamine
- Glass, crystal, ice, shard, tweak, crank, meth = methamphetamine—think of *AMC's* hit series, *Breaking Bad*
- Junk, smack, dope, black tar, or china white = heroin

God forbid if you find yourself in these types of situations; red-alert alarms should be clanging, and you need to make a break for it.

Need a way to make a break? Here's how you can get away from a Mr. Big Shot Drug Pusher.

Do you want to be an actress? Great. Be versatile and let's get on with this.

It's time to fire up your acting skills again.

Look at Mr. Power Player sweetly, but dead seriously. Politely ask him to get you a one-month supply of drugs. I repeat. Ask Mr. Big Shot for a one-month drug supply of blow, crank, X, smack, whatever, and watch his priceless reaction.

This asinine request should shock and scare the crap out of him. The last thing a Mr. Big Shot or Mr. Mega Celebrity needs is a crazed, whacked-out chick dying of a drug overdose on his property, and any bad press that will follow.

Remember for these narcissists, everything is about him.

If you do this, Mr. Big Shot will never offer you drugs again. That's exactly what you want.

On the other hand, if Mr. Big Shot gets you a 30-day supply of drugs, he's more warped and sadistically treacherous than you originally imagined.

Your only option is to get away from this sicko. Zoom.

Good girls don't do drugs and don't want anybody; no matter how famous or powerful they may be, offering them drugs either. After your outrageous one-month drug supply request, Mr. Big Shot may get a smidgen worried about your mental state, and give you a protein shake as he shoos you out the door.

Mission accomplished. Well done.

Drugs are a plague. They age you and turn Miss Fresh-Face into Miss Hag. Why give anybody the edge over you? The camera can be cruel.

Think about those close-up shots that will have to be heavily photo-shopped, and the auditions you missed, because you were too fucked up to go. Did you just blow what could have been your big break? Thanks to drugs you will never know.

Be grateful, and thank God, that you are not a drug addict that a powerful or famous dirtbag can take advantage of.

Help those who aren't as unfortunate.

LESSON #17: PARTIES! WHEN A PARTY IS A PARTY—WHEN A PARTY IS AN ORGY

Attention, aspiring actresses.

If you discover through one of Mr. Big Shot's mutual guy friend's that he is having a party that is news to you, do not throw a temper tantrum, and confront Mr. Big Shot demanding to know why you have not been invited.

Phew, thank God you were not invited.

Furthermore, don't jump the shark. Just don't, whatever you do, don't say anything stupid like this to him:

"What! You are having a party, and I'm not invited. Do I embarrass you? I'm living here at your house [or insert: "I thought we were friends" depending on your relationship with this Mr. Big Shot]. I don't understand."

Why? Because Mr. Big Shot will probably look at you with a piercing, detached coldness in his eyes, and tell you that he does not think that you are ready yet for *this kind of party*.

This kind of party is an orgy.

Oh. Oops. Stay with me, and pay close attention from here on out. Focus.

Orgies are sex parties that involve multiple sexual partners or group sex. People of every sexual orientation, and gender let loose, and engage in a hodgepodge of unrestrained sexual activities, gratification fantasies and fetishes with each other. Anything goes. There are no limits. It's like a Sodom and Gomorrah free-for-all.

Expect there to be drugs at an orgy and lots of them to choose from. Drugs numb people and eliminate their judgment by breaking down their boundaries so they will engage in sexual activities they would not do if they were not high. The more you do them, the less your conscience bothers you.

In addition, drugs disassociate a person's feelings to what is happening around them and *to them*.

It would not be a stretch to say there will be people at orgies who did not know what kind of party it was when they were invited. They thought attending a Hollywood party at a Mr. Power Player's mansion sounded like a super, cool time.

According to Wikipedia, the word *orgia* comes from ancient Greek. The goal of the orgia "was to achieve an ecstatic union with the divine." If violence was necessary to supposedly get there, so be it.

These Machiavellian orgy parties share a common bond of indecency, nasty sex, degrading sexual exploitation, and eroticism.

For a better view, think of Stanley Kubrick's movie, *Eyes Wide Shut,* starring Tom Cruise and Nicole Kidman.

Under the cover of darkness, the elite guests, cloaked in creepy masks and capes, like phantom of the opera wannabes, arrive at a majestic gated-estate in chauffeur driven cars, or limousines to participate in the orgy.

Wanting total secrecy, these well-heeled, perverted cowards (won't show your faces, huh, big shots?) require a secret password to give to security guards posted at the main entrance.

Once inside the mansion, ominous music is piped throughout the foyer, the corridors and various rooms.

The orgy is about to start, but first a ritual takes place. Masked women, the drugged-up sex slaves, wearing matching capes are standing in a robotic circular formation. The ritual involves chanting, howling and performing some whoring offering to an unknown deity or idol they are communicating with.

Then, simultaneously, the sex slaves drop their capes, revealing physically drop-dead gorgeous women underneath. The women are naked except for thongs, masks and towering high-heel stilettos. Next these naked women stand in a line reminiscent to a meat counter at a butchers shop for the picking.

Apart from an orgy's general awfulness, sadistic and risky sexual peculiarities are permissible and encouraged.

This explains (also from Wikipedia), how a guest at an orgy could be gangbanged—which used to be considered rape, and a crime, is now an accepted practice.

Being gangbanged is where a bunch of people are performing sex acts on one person either in turn (like a train), or at the same time.

The woman being gangbanged could be double penetrated by two different men—in two different orifices (vaginal and anal) or penetrated by two men in one orifice with sex toys, body parts, whatever.

As though blinded by external dark forces, people who attend these orgies claim what is brutal, evil, dehumanizing, agonizing, and traumatizing is good.

What used to be considered forbidden is now accepted as cool. Whips, chains, bondage paraphernalia ... what goes on at these revolting orgy parties is like turning a rock over in a sewer in hell. If you must know more, go to Wikipedia or other websites with orgy info if you can stomach it.

There are people who willingly participate in incredibly evil shit and call it fun. How can a person with a modicum of a conscience take pleasure and find euphoria in gangbanging?

Down, down, down you go.

It's a spiraling effect to the sewer until you are completely devoid of scruples trapped in the toxic swamp with no way out. Witness the destruction of morals.

There are parties, and there are orgies. You must be able to tell them apart.

Thank God Mr. Big Shot did not invite you to his orgy party, and you are reading this damnable book.

Who would want to be pimped out, and mercilessly passed around like a box of chocolates to masked men to be used, and abused, to fulfill their every twisted sexual fantasy and demented fetish? Talk about damaged goods. This world is like one diabolical masquerade, and when you turn around, there is another mask behind you ready to pounce and devour you.

Wake up, ladies. Get the stardust out of your eyes. This is serious shit.

The sooner you realize that an exclusive invitation from a Mr. Power Player or Mr. Movie Star to attend a private party at his estate that on the surface a million girls would die for may just kill you the better, and if you do survive.

You need to decide whether or not attending a life-altering orgy was worth the price of your soul, the years of therapy, and psychiatric examination you will eventually need to pull yourself together after being ripped apart. The repercussions are enormous.

Thank God you read this damnable book. You will not be duped into mixing them up. That's worth celebrating, right?

There are fun, harmless parties, and there are dehumanizing orgies.

You better know the difference.

Now you do.

LESSON #18: FRIENDLY REMINDER FOR POWERFUL DIRTBAGS

Attention, powerful and famous dirtbags. Remember the cautionary tale of Hollywood producer Don Simpson? If not, you should.

With a working-class start, once upon a time, Simpson was on top of the world.

He was Hollywood's golden boy.

He had it all.

Simpson used to be a part of the wildly successful, box-office powerhouse Don Simpson/Jerry Bruckheimer Films. They produced mega successful movies including *Top Gun* with Tom Cruise, *Beverly Hills Cop* with Eddie Murphy, *Dangerous Minds* with Russell Crow, and the surprise smash box office success, *Flashdance* starring Jennifer Beals.

That is until Simpson's proclivity for drugs, prostitutes, and everything nasty did him in when he was found dead of a drug overdose sitting on the toilet.[v]

Simpson was a known client of ex-con, Hollywood Madam Heidi Fleiss.

Fleiss was mentored by Beverly Hills Madame Alex until as Madame Alex described it to be, "the Whore Wars" occurred—when Heidi stole her "business, books, girls and guys."

As the *Los Angeles Times* reported, Madame Alex's "lucrative prostitution network catered to a private world of millionaire businessmen, movie stars, and Saudi Arabian sheiks," until Madame Alex was indicted on pandering charges.

For years, she had cooperated with law enforcement by sharing pillow talk info she had gotten from her girls she called her "creatures." Madame Alex has since died. [vi]

Fun, glamorous, right?

LESSON #19: ANOTHER FRIENDLY REMINDER FOR POWERFUL DIRTBAGS

You are not invincible.

Remember what happened to Charlie Miner, the smooth talking, prolific A & M record promoter?

Miner was behind pushing music artists like Janet Jackson, Sting, Bryan Adams, and Amy Grant to the top of the charts.

Miner lived the Hollywood dream.

He was also a party animal, who had it all until a jilted ex-lover, stripper shot him to death in his rented Malibu home as he was trying to slow down his lifestyle.

As the *Los Angeles Times* reported at the time, "Suzette McClure was thirty... and five feet two inches tall and weighed barely one hundred pounds.

She drove to Minor's beach house, pulled a .25-caliber semiautomatic from a fanny pack, and fired nine soft-point bullets - the kind that leave exit wounds the size of a grapefruit - into her former boyfriend." [vii]

Groovy, glamorous, right?

LESSON #20: SPOTTING THE CON ARTIST

L os Angeles attracts all walks of life. The brilliant, the talented, the gifted, the rich, the powerful, the famous, to the desperate, the broken, the con artist, the wannabes, the hanger-on, the faux mafia gangsters, the fake secret CIA spooks, the groupies, and the treacherous Yes-People.

Yes-People are bloodsucking parasites. Their sole purpose in life is to say "yes" to Mr. Movie Star, or Mr. Power Player, and suck up to them.

They will do and say anything to keep their jobs and the money flowing in their direction, and if that means propping up Mr. Movie Star instead of taking him to rehab when he needs drugs to keep functioning, they will do it. Think *HBO's* hit series, *Entourage.*

I digress, back to spotting the con artist.

Anybody can hop on a plane and land in Los Angeles. Anybody can a lease a Mercedes-Benz SLK, a racy Porsche, any upscale car. Anybody can purchase a couple sharp, well-tailored Armani suits, and print distinguished looking business cards that say in embossed letters "producer."

Anybody can say they have billionaire friends, or famous friends and promise you the world. Anybody can say they are somebody—that doesn't make it true.

Don't be naive. Con artists are the charmers and deceivers. The con artist is all flash with no there, there. They are the instant experts who are full of crap. Anyone can talk a big talk, but can they deliver?

It only takes a little time to expose a con artist. At any moment, the leasing company can repo their extravagant car. Watch what they do when the check comes at dinner at a trendy restaurant. Do they squirm, go to the bathroom, or pick up the check?

If a guy you suspect is a con artist, and claims he is in the film biz, look up his supposed credits on IMDb.com. At IMDb.com, you can confirm he's legit or expose him as a shyster in seconds.

Shhhh. It's a secret.

Beware of the con artists who skulk around at Alcoholic Anonymous (AA) meetings. These con artists pretend that they are recovering addicts to meet stars, and other Hollywood talent, who are in recovery, vulnerable and easy to exploit.

LESSON #21: JUST BECAUSE HE'S A COUNT OR A LORD DOESN'T MEAN HE'S ROYAL

If a flirty-but-sweet party girl, tells you something like this, shrieking like a hysterical teenager, "OMG. I just met a Lord. A real life Lord and me! He asked me for my number. He wants to get to know me better. Can you believe it?"

The party girl's veins are popping out. She's hyperventilating now, "I mean, you know. I mean, you know. OMG!! I can't believe it. A royal, a royal ... OMG! It's so awesome. He has friends. They are Counts. Isn't that awesome? Do you want me to introduce you to him so you can meet a Count?" Tell her to get a grip and to breathe. Chill out.

It's La-La Land where anything goes, and everything is for sale, and that includes buying a royal title.

Some people refer to them as elite titles. That's right. This is not the bloodlines of the United Kingdom's House of Windsor we're talking about either.

So, let's see what the real deal is. Are royal titles are for sale? Check. Are blood tests required? No. That's right, babe. It's about image, image, image, and the appearance of status, status, status.

"Lord," "Barron," "Count" and "Duke," pick a title any title. You can buy a royal title online like purchasing a Prada bucket bag at the Prada e-store. You can buy a title and give it as a birthday gift to a friend. Go online, and Google, "buy royal or noble titles," and see what the going rates are.

While having a royal title before your name is a superficial boost on the rise to phony prominence, good girls do not have to be hoodwinked by counterfeits who abuse this impressive illusion because they know better. They have read this damnable book.

Bought-and-paid-for titles come with bells and whistles including in the form of paperwork, like a Certificate, Crescent and the Title Deed of Assignment. Some titles are shipped off in leather bound Manorial Medieval 12th Century style cases.

If you meet a Count Big Shot or a Lord Power Player, and he invites you to his place during the day (Lesson #2), and he pulls out his royal title paperwork. He is using it as a prop to bedazzle you.

If he then attempts to lure you into his imperial bed, now you know the deal, and you can be de-dazzled.

Props like this have been known in La-la-land to be called a pussy trap. Sound crude?

Yes. It is. Get over it. That's what they are.

Another popular pussy trap to entice Miss Ingénue into the sack is to showcase pictures of Mr. Power Player, or Count Big Shot, with celebrities.

These celebrity photos can be hanging framed on their walls, rotating in a slideshow in electronic, digital photo frames, or be arranged neatly in photo albums that he pulls out to show you.

"Look at me with [insert Mr. Movie Star's name here]."

Watch Miss Ingénue's eyes get all big and wide.

If this happens to you, what Mr. Power Player is saying is if you are nice to him, and if you are his special girl, he will introduce you to his very good friends, [insert Mr. Movie Stars names here].

Royal titles and celebrity photographs make outstanding pussy traps. They are effective props to woo the pants off of star-struck neophytes who aren't hip to the game.

These young women fatally believe they will get closer to making their dreams of stardom into a reality if they hook up with these dirtbags in the sack.

The bottom line?

Pussy traps increase a power player's odds of getting a young, sexy promising actress to open her legs for him. That's the intent and the whole point of having pussy traps. Get it? To get a girl in the sack! You need to know about pussy traps so you won't get ensnared in one.

But I digress. Enough about pussy traps.

Let's go back to the splendid topic of royal titles, shall we?

For your information, it is good to know that companies who sell royal titles do try hard to avoid selling duplications, or selling you a title that belongs to another person who is still alive.

It sucks when that happens, but mistakes do occur. If you decide to go royal title shopping, be sure to do your due diligence first.

So the next time you meet a Count or Lord or whatever royal title some guy is throwing around like confetti, while you are having a blast at another *Vanity Fair* soiree; know this. You can buy a royal title too, and in short order, be called a Lady, a Countess, or Duchess.

Just like Lord Big Shot, you can have fawning sycophants bowing or curtsying at your feet. Oh, my my my.

Royal titles are just not that special anymore.

LESSON #22: IF A CELEBRITY GETS A STAR ON THE HOLLYWOOD WALK OF FAME IT DOESN'T MEAN THEY ARE TALENTED

It is not simply royal titles that are for sale, but you can buy a star on the Hollywood Walk of Fame too. What? Didn't you know that? Yes, you can. To get the latest prices, call the Mayor's office.

Surprised?

Did you think it was a fluke, or a twist of fate, thanks to the magical sun gods, when celebrities receive a star on the Hollywood Walk of Fame, that it coincides with a highly anticipated movie premiere, or an album release? No, it's not a coincidence. It's rigged and orchestrated. It's called stagecraft and theatrics at a price.

Honestly, take the blinders off.

Look at the list of Hollywood Walk of Fame recipients. Hugh Hefner, the founder of *Playboy,* and puppets, like Kermit the Frog? A puppet? Oh, the astonishing deception of it all.

Sharpen up, ladies.

Getting a star on the Hollywood Walk of Fame is about optics. It's a lucrative publicity stunt and the fans totally eat it up. The sooner you realize that everything is for sale in Hollywood the better off you will be.

If you have the dough, you can buy a star, a royal title, anything, and everything, you can think of.

The days of earning a star on the Hollywood Walk of Fame because of real talent, and extraordinary contribution to cinema, are long gone. That distinction and honor was sold out for cash a long time ago.

However, if you get an invite to attend a Hollywood Walk of Fame Star unveiling—go and don't miss the party afterwards. There's plenty of deelish food and amusing festivities to enjoy. It's a great network opportunity to boot. Bring business cards with you and work it.

Don't forget to take the swag bag.

Swag bags are like loot bags for kids except they're an adult version. They are overloaded with neat stuff like skin care products, electronics, latest gadgets, spa treatments certificates and a smorgasbord of other goodies for celebrities to try.

Take one. Take two (if you can). Enjoy!

You know what the real deal is because you read this damnable book.

Don't take this manufactured Hollywood smoke and mirrors crap so seriously.

Have fun and work it.

LESSON #23: IF A CREEPY GUY TRIES TO RECRUIT YOU TO GO OVERSEAS TO MODEL...

It's after work. Happy-hour time. There you are minding your business, sipping on a tasty cosmopolitan, at the Beverly Hills Hotel Polo Longue bar, waiting for a friend to arrive.

Suddenly some creepy guy saunters over to you, and begins to tell you how remarkably beautiful you are. He is not very tall, but sharply dressed.

Mr. Creepy Guy asks, "Are you a model? You so pretty."

The man, who is not American, has a deep voice, heavy accent, and speaks in hushed tones.

"So, sweetheart, you like to travel?"

Listen intently to Mr. Creepy Guy go on because despite his stilted delivery, his pitch for you to travel to some faraway place initially sounds exotic and exciting.

It's amusing in that appalling kind of way. The more he talks, the more wound up he becomes. You will begin to wonder if he has recited this script a million times.

As Mr. Creepy Guy tells the story, he's a talent scout who works for a deep-pocketed mysterious, prominent man in the Middle East.

He's looking for models to fly over for an all-expense paid modeling junket. Mr. Creepy Guy throws around crazy-high money numbers that he claims you will be paid to model for a few weeks. He promises that you will be treated like a princess, and see things that you have never seen before.

"Everything is First Class. First Class all the way," Mr. Creepy Guy repeats for extra emphasis. "You so pretty. You like First Class, sweetheart?" he asks continuing to pile on the flattery. "You sparkle like diamonds. Anybody tell you that before, sweetheart? You like diamonds? We have diamonds. You like jewelry? We pay bonuses in jewelry for special job well done. Only the best for such a beautiful woman like you."

If this happens to you, Mr. Creepy Guy is recruiting you, like a pimp.

Recruiters are paid heaps of cash for every girl they send overseas to astonishingly, wealthy men, some who are allegedly part of a Royal family to "model."

Some of the women come back. Others don't. Women who bite the bait are bought and sold. Getting on a plane and going anywhere this creepy guy plans to send you would be a hallucinatory exercise if you thought it would end well.

If this happens to you, get all wide-eyed, and ask Mr. Creepy Guy lots of questions and details. Which country? Is he a prince? A Sheik, a Sultan? What's a Sultan (play dumb)? How many weeks? How much money will I get paid each week? What about my down time? Can I leave the compound? Ooh and ahh a lot.

Just when Mr. Creepy Guy thinks he's reeled you in, so he can ship you off to a faraway place to God-knows-who to do God-knows-what, tell him that you are a journalist, and to bug off.

Oh shit.

Watch Mr. Creepy Guy skedaddle away.

He will never bother you again.

Nice one.

Well done.

LESSON #24: HAIR PLUGS, PENIS IMPLANTS, INTRAVENOUS VITAMINS, AND THAT MYSTERIOUS BRAIN MACHINE

D o you think it is just women who are vain? Think again. There's nothing more annoying than a guy who takes longer to get dressed than you do—even if he is an impossibly charming Mr. Movie Star.

Los Angeles is full of delusion, and egomania, where people are always chasing the fountain of youth.

This vanity epidemic is a LA crisis not just for women, but for men too.

This is why there is the prevalent use of hair plugs, penis implants, intravenous vitamins, and sightings of that mysterious brain machine.

Do I need to say more here? Really? Yes, I must? Okay, fine.

You got me. It is true. Mr. Big Celebrity uses them all—or a combination of them, especially when a Mr. Rock Star is on tour. They also put lifts in their shoes.

And that mysterious brain machine... If you have never seen one, it is not very big. It is smaller than your average microwave oven for easy travel use with connected attachments that you stick on your head. The mysterious brain machine activates, and opens up areas of the brain that the average person never uses... as the story goes.

Being Mr. Rock Star is not easy.

It's a tough grind traveling all day, performing all night, then being the life of the party at the groupie bash backstage after the concert, and beyond as you sing around the world.

Holy moly! The mysterious brain machine—it's about stamina, baby, stamina. It can work in concert with the penis implant.

Pun intended! Rock on.

LESSON #25: GIFTS THAT TELL YOU MR. RICH OR FAMOUS IS A SUPER FREAK

If you recently met a Mr. Power Player or Mr. Movie Star and you are visiting him at his place, in the day time (Lesson #2), and he tells you that he has a present for you. Then he asks you what size you are—this is a red flag.

You hesitate, but you give him your size as requested. If moments later Mr. Big Shot presents you with a gift, and it is some type of clothing like a sexy maid's outfit, lingerie, or silk pajamas, he's a super freak, and, oh, by the way, you are also not special.

This is not a gag gift either. He is serious.

Think about it.

If Mr. Big Shot has your present in different sizes hanging in one of his closets; imagine how many other special women like you received the same sexually-charged, tacky gift. Ick.

What the heck? This guy is such a pathetic loser.

What does Mr. Power Player or Mr. Movie Star think you are going to do with his gift?

I will tell you what.

He's expecting you to gush, thank him profusely, and insist on trying on the sexy outfit to model for him. This way he can see how well it fits on your voluptuous body. That's what.

This kind of tawdry assembly-line gift giving practice also applies to Mr. Big Shots' who give necklaces with a cross-shaped pendant with a single jewel in the center.

If you are a recipient of one of these, did Mr. Big Shot tell you with a straight face that the Pope blessed it when he gave it to you, and only to you because you are so damn special?

Sharpen up, ladies. Have you learned nothing yet? This is not some screwball comedy.

This is the glamorous Hollywood life.

It's downright idiotic.

If you believe Mr. Big Shot's BS, and you proudly wear the necklace, and brag about the Pope's blessing, don't be surprised when you bump into another women at a nightclub saying the same thing while wearing the same cross necklace with a different color stone. Red for ruby, green for emerald, blue for topaz... You get the picture, right?

If nothing else, these Mr. Power Players are consistent and have no shame.

They are always on the prowl.

Take your gift, head for the door.

Have a good laugh with some friends and never call these clowns again.

LESSON #26: SLUTTY TRAMPS AND BARBIE-DOLL BIMBOS

If you dress like a slutty tramp in Hollywood, you will be treated like a slutty trap.

While these women give all women a bad name, not all women are slutty tramps, Barbie-doll bimbos, gold diggers, vamps, or desperate to be famous.

Not all women are whoring their way up the casting couch ladder to get to the supposed top of the stardom pyramid.

Good girls do not flaunt their bodies to get attention. They keep it classy and have self-respect. Good girls have a hard enough time being taken seriously, thanks to slutty tramps, and Barbie-doll bimbos, who give all women a bad name.

Women who walk around like slutty tramps only attract negative attention.

Perhaps they might acquire some short-term monetary gain.

Conversely, depending on where you are going, like to a nightclub, or to the haunted Chateau Marmont, for drinks, it is not always a bad idea to hang out with a couple slutty tramps or Barbie-doll bimbos.

Why?

Because they act like living dirtbag screeners and they don't even know it. Meow. Sounds catty and vicious, right ladies? No. It's the truth.

If a Mr. Big Celebrity hits on a slutty tramp or Barbie-doll bimbo, he is not someone you want to know, or get involved with. Why bother with this dirtbag?

Slutty tramps, or Barbie-doll bimbos, will save you headaches and heartaches in the long run as dirtbag screeners. They instantly expose the content of the mega-powerful or famous' character.

Let them steal the scene.

Is Mr. Power Player, or Mr. Movie Star, salivating, drooling, and slobbering like a bulldog?

Is he asking the slutty tramp or Barbie-doll bimbo what color they would like for a Mercedes two-seater they swear they are going to give them (but never do)? If so, Mr. Big Shot is looking for another woman to add to his late night call Rolodex-rotation (Lesson #2). That's it.

Hint. Hint. Get my meaning now?

Does that sound bitchy or provocative?

Try it, and you'll see what I mean, and why it's true. It works, and remember, *I told you so.*

While slutty tramps, and Barbie-doll bimbos, do provide this vital dirtbag screening public service, be careful not to hang out with too many of them because you are judged by the company you keep.

Good girls show a little cleavage, or some leg, but never both. Leave something to the imagination, ladies, please.

If you are walking around virtually naked in your birthday suit what are you going to do next for an encore performance? Get more extreme that's what.

The Soft Porn Music Industry

Look at the evolution to the dark side that is now the music industry full of pop tarts looking like slutty tramps, or Barbie-doll bimbos. This is a tale of what used to be companies, and talented music artists, creating and selling music, and well, entertaining people around the world.

Today the music biz has turned into a pervasive soft porn factory. It churns out smutty, debauched videos, vulgar concerts, and promiscuous lyrics that are polluting innocent kids and teenagers' minds under the guise of entertainment.

Kids are being sexualized, and conditioned, by today's pop tarts to embrace, and imitate, a soft porn culture, and to dress like slutty tramps and Barbie-doll bimbos.

While sex has always sold, there used to be a level of respect, decency and mystery. Today that has vanished—anything goes.

Why do you think female pop artists music videos become raunchier, more erotic, and risqué with each new release?

Look at me! Look at me!

Soon there will be no other body parts left to shove and grind into a camera lens to broadcast to the world. It's become a race to the gutter. Empowering, right?

And the fallout? Reportedly, there has been a "severe epidemic" of sexually transmitted diseases sweeping the nation. Singers should be singers and not act like fluffers.

Don't know what a fluffer is?

Fluffers are women who get men sexually fired up and keep their dicks hard. As the illustrious urban dictionary notes, a fluffer is a girl who "gives head to the porn stars behind the camera to keep the guys hard."[viii] That's right, the dick sucking warm-up act that doesn't make the silver screen.

Don't be a fluffer.

Moreover, someone needs to tell fluffers that being known as a blowjob queen for whatever reason is not a badge of honor. You can consult with former *CBS News* anchor Katie Couric. She was recently quoted as saying, "I wonder who she blew *this* time to get it," referring to Diane Sawyer and an interview she landed.[ix]

You don't have to be an investigative journalist to know the deal.

Ladies have some self-respect. Keep your clothes on, your legs closed, and your ass out of other people's faces.

Thanks.

LESSON #27: TRIVIAL PIECE OF IMPORTANT INFORMATION

While they might look cool, Lamborghinis suck. Have you ever tried getting out of a Lamborghini wearing Manolo Blahnik 6-inch high heels? There is nothing luxurious, or elegant, about needing a crane to pull you out of a low-riding Lamborghini.

LESSON #28: HOW TO BLOW OFF MR. MARRIED POWER PLAYER AFTER HE MAKES A PLAY FOR YOU

The male ego is fragile. You've got to constantly stroke it. For a Mr. Big Shot, or Mr. Mega Celebrity, it requires much more stroking than the average Joe. Their egos are on steroids because it is constantly pumped up by people (and the dastardly Yes-People), who blow smoke up their asses hoping to get a piece of their money, fame and power.

Consequently, Mr. Power Player and Mr. Movie Star are not used to anyone saying no to them—even if they hit on you and they are married men.

If a Mr. Married Big Shot, or Mr. Married Movie Star, hits on you, and you turn him down, as far as they are concerned, you are the one with the problem and not them. Right ladies?

Married men who cheat on their wives always whine the same stupid, sucky sob-story that has nothing to with you. *Their wives treat them dreadfully. They are so lonely.* Boohoo.

Maybe their wives treat them terribly because they screw around, and cannot be trusted out of view in a range any further than 5-feet away.

On the other hand, if it's not the my-wife-treats-me-dreadfully sucky, sob story, it's the I'm in an open marriage spiel. Supposedly that makes it okay to jump in the sack with him. Really?

And being with a married man in an open marriage should be appealing because everyone wants to be with a swinger?

Who wants to run to the doctor's office every time they are with Mr. Open-Marriage Power Player to get checked out for STD (Sexual Transmitted Disease)? This is supposed to be a turn-on? Pulease.

These men are jackasses and self-possessed idiots— rich or poor. If you are unhappily married get a divorce before you start making moves on other women.

How hard is that to understand?

Good girls can work with, and be friends with a married man, and they never play with another woman's husband.

If a married man cannot be friends, or work with a single woman, that speaks volumes for his lack of character.

When Mr. Married Big Shot makes a pass at you, here is how to let him down gently to see if it is possible to remain friends, or if his wounded ego wins out.

You say you want to be an actress? Turn up your acting skills and bring on the tears.

Tell Mr. Married Big Shot that you are greedy. You could never share him with another person because the time apart from him while knowing he was with (Insert Mr. Big Shot's wife name here) would be tortuous and painful. This will lessen the rejection blow to his ego. This way you are flattering him while you are rejecting him.

Say something like this:

"I want you as much as you want me but I can't share you—it would kill me. If I can't have you all to myself, I can't have you at all. I couldn't stand being apart from you at Christmas, your birthday..."

Mr. Married Big Shot will be touched. If he is not a total jerk and scumbag— and this is a work situation, you may not lose your job. It's worth giving it a try because the alternative is having sex with him to keep it temporarily, and that's not going to happen.

Once you reject Mr. Married Man's sexual advances in a social setting; don't expect to hear from him in the immediate future. His ego is wounded, and he is out looking for fresh prey. That will change in about six months.

After a few months, if you call him, he will call you back because you are a challenge, and for the sake of his ego, he will try to make another play for you.

It may take years, but one day these powerful married men will give up trying to bed you, wave the white flag. Then, and only then will he be able to be friends because he respects you.

The problem all along is that he does not respect himself.

LESSON #29: WHAT IS A FIXER?

Fixers are hired-guns who cleanup Mr. Movie Star's personal messes, or indiscretions, that could turn into an international media frenzy if the truth got out to the press.

Naturally, some of the messes involve Miss One Night Stand or Miss Ex-Girlfriend.

In Hollywood there are four types of fixers: the high-priced lawyers, the unsuspecting publicist/management assistants, bodyguards and thugs.

Beware.

What a mega celebrity needs to be "fixed" could be virtually anything. It might be as simple as a movie star needing a speeding ticket fixed, or he might need a woman hushed up because he gave her herpes.

Maybe Mr. Movie Star does not want it known that he had a penis implant operation which Miss Ex-Girlfriend can confirm since she was there before and after the delicate procedure.

There is a whole host of reasons why Mr. Movie Star is trying to shut up a woman, who only weeks earlier he had professed his undying love for.

Fixer #1: The high-priced lawyer. These legal eagle fixers have been known to intimidate Miss Ex-Girlfriend or Miss One Night Stand into signing confidentiality agreements, or cease and desist orders. Especially if she has been contacted by the tabloids or *she contacted* the tabloids. The double-barrel fixer stories of celebrity lawyers are legendary.

Blackmail is a favorite tool to help incentivize cooperation from a disgruntled woman. This is where all those sexually provocative photos, and sex tapes you posed in, and filmed can come back to haunt you.

Of course, Hollywood's fancy, high-priced lawyers, in crisp, pressed suits don't call it blackmail because that would be illegal. As officers of the court, they would never do anything illegal, right (wink)?

The phrase, "You'll never work in this town again," is another tactic they like to pull.

It's called getting blackballed. Fixers play dirty because there's a lot at stake for them. They charge mega stars' hefty bucks for their services and want to keep that money train chugging along.

And if all that fails, high-priced lawyers will hire private investigators to dig up dirt to use against women by enlisting the freelance help of Fixer # 3 and #4.

A little payola could come into play here too.

The onetime flamboyant PI to the stars and mega-powerful, Anthony Pellicano is a perfect example of a fixer in action.

Pellicano is sitting in a jail cell after being found guilty of racketeering charges. He terrorized people (illegal wiretapping, dead fish on car windshields...) who were problems for the mega-powerful and famous for years.[x]

Fixer #2: The unsuspecting assistants' who work at hotshot public relation firms or management companies that represent celebrities.

Surely, it must have come as a shock the first time when an assistant's well-heeled boss summoned them into their plush office. Shut the door behind them and told them about an urgent, secret task that needed to be done immediately. *Absolute discretion is required. This is really important. I am counting on you here.*

The important, highly-confidential task was to drive Miss One Night Stand to an abortion clinic to get an abortion, and then take her home to recover after it was complete. Oh, no. One of their Mr. Mega Celebrity clients knocked up the young girl.

What?! You want me to do what?! Take [insert Mr. Movie Star's name here] latest squeeze for an abortion!

I know you thought that when you landed this terrific assistant's job at a prestigious firm you thought you would be exposed to a fabulous life of glitz and glamour.

Of course, you knew there would be some humdrum work, like answering phones, pouring coffee, picking up dry cleaning, ordering the car service... but you never imagined abortion clinic trips.

That's right. This fixer task may apply to other entertainment biz assistants, who work at movie studios and top-notch celebrity talent agencies.

These assistants, like those at the pr/management firms, had no idea either that they would be enlisted as a part of the fixer duties when they landed their killer job.

While it is true that "abortion clinic trips" are not listed in the job details description in the classified sections of the *Hollywood Reporter*, *Variety* (known as the rags) and the *Los Angeles Times*, apparently these duties fall under the run errands job requirement.

Fixer #3: The bodyguard. Some celebrities and their lawyers hire ex-cops as part of their security detail. These guys might be called in to fix a problem.

Fixer #4: The thug. The thug is the scariest fixer of them all. Thugs are paid henchmen.

Some thugs are drug addicts. Drug addicts will do anything for a hit off the crack pipe. Anything. Usually, thugs travel in packs and have a willing posse of pals with similar addictions.

Their posse will help fix any scandalous problems Mr. Power Player or Mr. Movie Star may have gotten into. No rules apply.

You have been warned.

LESSON #30: FLASHBULBS—HOW TO DEAL WITH THE MEDIA

If the *National Enquirer,* or any media outlet, contacts you, you better call them back to see what they want. If you don't, they will "report" whatever they want.

Tape the conversation (California is a two party state, so you need to tell the person that you are taping them), or take notes. This way if a press person edits and distorts your words you can correct it ideally both with the paper's editor and your website.

Yes, you must have your own website.

It's your platform to market yourself and your skills. Don't be afraid if you are attacked in the press. It is a great opportunity to fight back and correct them. Threats and insults should not bother you.

Look at the source of where they are coming from. Does someone want to throw mud at you? Big deal. Throw a boatload of mud right back at them. Two can play this game, and Mr. Mega Celebrities have much more to lose than you do.

So don't be intimidated. Always keep titillating proof, so you have a couple aces in your back pocket—if you need them.

They do so why shouldn't you? Document. Document. Document.

If possible, try to develop relationships with gossip columnists. Leaking stories to them can come in handy, and is a good insurance policy to keep Mr. Big Shots in-line, who cross the line. But beware; Mr. Power Player and Mr. Movie Star have gossip columnist contacts too. They aren't afraid to play let's-make-a-deal to try to silence you by promising press people future exclusive scoops (Lesson #29).

Snakes, right?

LESSON #31: MAKING BOOK

Whoops! Oh, so you thought this lesson was about booking a job, and how to prepare when you receive slides from a casting director for a TV or film role audition to book a job? Slides are part of a script actors receive to rehearse a role they are being considered to play. Book it?

Think again.

This lesson is about bookies, slang for bookmakers. You know the gambling guys you see at the race track, fights and sporting events, Vegas and places like that who take bets at agreed upon odds?

Bookies don't place bets for themselves; they make money when gamblers place bets with them on what is known as a transaction fee—"the vig."

They also lend money to gamblers and have outstanding dirt on everybody who likes to gamble. Bookies know who has real money and who are the loud-mouthed, flat-broke frauds living the smoke and mirrors LA life.

Bookies make for excellent, fun friends with wicked, hilarious stories. Despite their somewhat menacing appearance and bad reputations, many bookies have an endearing soft spot.

The good news is they play by a code of ethics and hold true to them.

You lose a bet you pay. You place a bet, and you pay the vig. It's not rocket science. Play by the rules. Period.

Bookies also have deadbeat gambling clients who owe them money.

A bookmaker's client list includes everybody and anybody from doctors, dentists, car dealership owners, Mr. Big Shots and Mr. Movie Stars.

Knowing a bookie is especially handy if you don't have health, or dental insurance, or if your car breaks down, and the warranty expired.

Bookies always get paid one way or another, and they love to call in debts.

And if that means your bookie pal sends you to one of his deadbeat doctor clients for a check-up, or dentist for a teeth cleaning, or to a car dealership owner to get your car fixed to collect a debt, consider it done.

There is that neat, super nice, and painless way for bookies to collect a debt from deadbeat bettors and, oh, there's that kneecap thing too.

LESSON #32: MODELING GIG AT A RANCH WITH A HOLLYWOOD TV EVANGELIST

The fake Christian racket for profit is nothing new, so it should not come as a surprise that there are fake Christians in California, seeking fame, stardom and fortune while they blaspheme God's word and pass the donation plate around the congregation.

The best way to know if a person is a fake is by witnessing how they live when the cameras or microphones are turned off. Do they practice what they preach?

Enter the Hollywood dark side scenario—evangelist style.

Let's say your new agent books you on a modeling gig to be on a cable TV show, starring a Mr. Hollywood Evangelist that is filmed on location at his sprawling ranch outside of Los Angeles.

Sounds like fun, and you get paid, right?

You are thrilled, delighted and excited. It's incredible. Your agent told you that for $1000 a day for ten days all you have to do is ride horses and play tennis.

You can't believe your good fortune after all this time struggling and trying to make ends meet. $1,000 a day! This is your big break. You feel like you have hit the lottery.

After ten days of modeling at the ranch, you can finally afford to buy some furniture to go with the futon you've been sleeping on in that tiny studio apartment you rented with your best friend in Westwood.

Let's face it, moving to Los Angeles has been challenging since you both packed up all your worldly possessions and crammed them into the used Hyundai and road tripped it straight from South Dakota to sunny California.

Isn't LA great? $1,000 a day to ride horses and play tennis!

Slow down. Yeah, right.

No one pays $1,000 just to ride horses or play tennis. Not even a Christian, God fearing Mr. Hollywood Evangelist (wink, wink).

If that were true, I would not be sitting here writing this damnable book. I would be having the time of my life soaking up rays while riding horses and playing tennis with Mr. Hollywood Evangelist.

Some clichés withstand the test of time.

When it sounds too good to be true, it is.

Sure, Mr. Hollywood Evangelist likes to ride horses. He loves his horses. There is even a camera crew filming up-and-coming models on horses at his ranch for cheesy b-roll for his cable TV show, but Mr. Hollywood Evangelist also wants to ride you.

Hey. Don't despair. It's not all bad news from here. Good girls don't have to miss all the fun because you know the drill now.

Anything can be lucrative for a short time (Lesson #11). Go to the ranch in your used Hyundai until you get kicked out for not putting out and have fun!

The length of time you can spend at the ranch all depends on your acting skills and the tools you have learned to use by reading this damnable book.

How long can you keep this gig going until Mr. Hollywood Evangelist gets frustrated with you because you won't open your legs and take him for a ride?

Will it be one, two or three-days until he replaces you with another model that is willing to ride him bareback?

The good news is Mr. Hollywood Evangelist has a public image to maintain. The deep-pocket charlatan certainly doesn't need any embarrassing rumors, or press leaking out about what is going on at his ranch being a Christian, man of God and all that crap.

Eventually, Mr. Hollywood Evangelist will have no choice but to accept that you went to his ranch to do the job you were hired to do, and that's it. He will cut his modeling booking contract with you short and send you home early with a pay to-go-away check.

Big deal.

Take the check for the work you were booked to do, say thank you and wave good-bye.

Wasn't that the easiest $2,000-$4,000 you've earned in a long time? You can still buy a few things for your studio apartment and save the rest for a rainy day, and most importantly, unlike Mr. Hollywood Evangelist, your soul is intact.

You did not succumb to the Hollywood temptations and sell-out like he did.

Congratulations!

Pray for Mr. Hollywood Evangelist masquerading as a good Christian to correct the errors of his ways and to seek redemption. A dirtbag is a dirtbag.

Mr. Hollywood Evangelist needs to get right with the living God, pronto.

When you get home from the ranch, give your new agent the axe.

Getting paid to go away is nothing new. It happens all the time in the corporate world with Mr. Wall Street. It's called the golden parachute.

Ace!

LESSON #33: THE THREE-DAY TRAVEL RULE

If a Mr. Power Player invites you to accompany him on a trip, say to Las Vegas, New York City, Lake Tahoe, or San Francisco, for some harmless gambling or to catch a show and some dinner. Always be clear about the status of your relationship before you go.

Are you travelling as friends or as lovers?

Nobody likes being taken advantage of so don't do it to anyone either.

Set the boundaries before you leave for the airport. Know where you stand. If you are not interested in Mr. Power Player romantically and see him as a friend, tell him. This way if any funny business starts after the plane takes off, he can't accuse you of leading him on.

Ask Mr. Power Player about the accommodations for your trip. Will you have your own hotel room or will you be sharing one suite with separate bedrooms with him and so forth?

Mini vacations with Mr. Power Player or Mr. Movie Star rock and are full of decadent fun.

Many luxury suites at 5-star hotels or resorts have a.m. and p.m. butlers on duty to cater to your every whim—this could be a real-life princess experience for you. Butlers can have a warm bath ready with orchids floating in the water for you if you tell them what time you will be back in the room.

That being said, if it has been established that you are traveling as friends know that could change after the airplane takes off.

Without warning, the cool Mr. Power Player, you thought was a trustworthy gentleman, who said he enjoyed your company, and promised that you were travelling as friends, turns into a sick, sadistic bastard.

"You are not in your territory anymore," Mr. Power Player or Mr. Movie Star abruptly growled at you with a salivating look in his steely eyes, "You are in mine." Boom!

Oh shit.

Big bone-chilling shudder here.

This is mortifying. Mr. Power Player has just sandbagged you. You are not close to home. There is no quick exit door, and you don't need to get into a sparring match with this cretin.

Immediately say this to try to knock some sense into him and keep him at arm's length:

"I can't believe you just did that to me. I'm somebody's daughter too! If some guy did to your daughter what you just tried to do to me, you'd shoot off his knee caps."

Rewind.

Of course, maybe that won't happen, everything will be fine, and this trip will be another entertaining chapter to add to your book, but just in case, here's how to avoid that kind of a dreadful situation from the get-go.

It is called the three-day travel rule.

The three-day travel rule is simple.

Don't travel anywhere with a Mr. Big Shot or Mr. Movie Star for one day longer than three days. That's three days, not four days, not five days, but three days. That means two nights. Are we clear?

Suffice to say that if Mr. Big Shot decides to change the platonic rules, you can keep his sexual advances at bay for two nights.

After that it gets tricky and very, very uncomfortable, even with a.m. and p.m. butlers a buzzer push away to cater to your every desire.

You are not in your territory anymore. You are in mine.

For two nights, all men will believe that you are menstruating which is precisely what you will point out to Mr. Big Shot before the plane takes off.

How do you do that? By offhandedly mentioning that you have your period by referring to being bloated or having some cramps, but a trip any longer than the three-day-two-night duration and your mini vacation could turn into one hell of a nightmare.

For reasons unknown, Mr. Power Players and Mr. Movie Stars can become delusional.

They always believe they can change your mind and seduce you into their beds after the plane takes off.

I don't know why this happens.

Maybe it is the altitude. That's why the three days-two nights trip is your safest bet.

Do you see the beautiful logic behind that now?

Go and have fun on your three-day-two-night mini vacation. Don't forget to take the shampoo samples and other amenities in your hotel room when you leave. They come in handy when money is tight, and most importantly, don't forget to pack some tampons and maxi pads before you go even if it is not that time of the month.

Bon voyage.

LESSON #34: IF YOU BROKE THE THREE-DAY TRAVEL RULE

So you have decided to ignore the masterful three-day travel rule.

You have agreed to go on a trip with Mr. Power Player or Mr. Movie Star for longer than three days. You are excited because you have never been to the Cannes Film Festival, skiing in Aspen, San Tropez, Hong Kong, the Caribbean, Belize, wherever.

Besides, traveling is on your bucket list of things to do.

You tell yourself that it would be nuts to turn down such a great opportunity to travel with an important, influential man.

How could you turn down a first-class, all- expenses-paid-for trip like that? It's an opportunity of a lifetime you rationalize.

Okay, fine. Be like that. Don't say I didn't warn you.

If it has been established that you are traveling platonically, no romance or sex, breaking the three-day travel rule requires additional preparation.

It is time to activate your acting skills again.

You can prep Mr. Power Player to keep his hands off you like this.

A couple of days before you are scheduled to leave town with him, tell Mr. Power Player that you were rear ended while driving to the gym. Luckily it was not a serious bender fender, and you can still go on the trip, but you are a little sore and stiff.

Okay, that's a lie, but do you want to outrun Mr. Big Shot or not in the event he goes grab-happy psycho on you?

After you leave on your voyage and get settled into the 5-star resort, when you know Mr. Big Shot is due back at your hotel suite, lie down on the floor on your back. Put your knees up with your feet pressed to your bum like a triangle.

This is a position a doctor recommends for people to get into to help alleviate their back pain.

When Mr. Big Shot comes into the room and sees you on the floor, complaining about the pain, he will be afraid to touch you.

Even better he might send you to the spa for a deep tissue or Swedish massage to help you feel better and to work out the kinks in your back. Also refer to Lesson #11 for additional tips.

More Travel Tips

Before you go on a trip with Mr. Big Shot or Mr. Movie Star tell friends and family where you are going, where you will be staying and when you will be back.

Don't you dare leave, especially if you going out of the country, without having the contact information to the U.S. Embassy.

Also get a list of cheap hotels or youth hostels where you can flee if you've got to split.

Hopefully, this will not be necessary, but if Mr. Power Player turns ugly, you can avoid being at his mercy by having a Plan B. Always, always keep your return ticket and passport nearby.

If all that fails and you need to gross him out, ask him if he's seen gonorrhea or syphilis of the mouth? That should turn him off, at least for a little while as you plot your escape.

The bottom line is this. You need to decide if rolling the dice by traveling with someone you don't know that well is worth the risk.

Hell, in just a few short years if you keep working hard, you can travel on your dime.

Red Alert Warning for Overseas Modeling Gigs

While there are legitimate overseas modeling gigs around the world in places like Japan, Europe, the Middle East and Caribbean islands, there are also modeling gigs that involve much more than modeling in these locations and elsewhere that are sketchy, if not downright dangerous.

You must proceed with caution.

Before you pack your bags with dollar signs and visions of impressive tear sheets in your eyes, speak to other women who have gone to the same place. They will tell you what goes on under the guise of "modeling."

If anybody warns you not to go, you must pay attention to their warning. Your experience will not be better or different than theirs was—it could be worse.

The sex trafficking business is real and deadly. Google "modeling agency and sex trafficking" to get a taste for what is out there. This is no joke. Women have been held hostage by phony modeling agencies and disappeared, never to be seen again.

In these dramatic tragedies, the story-line and the plots are always the same; only the women come and go.

Know this.

Any modeling job where the people running it hold onto your passport during the course of your contract is a no-go zone.

I don't care how much money they are offering to pay you. You are headed for a disaster. Don't go.

End of discussion.

LESSON #35: MEETING MR. BIG CELEB

C ontrary to conventional wisdom, meeting celebrities is easy. They might seem larger than life and untouchable on the big screen but when you are in Los Angeles, it's not hard to run into them.

When you encounter Mr. Movie Star or Mr. Rock Star, never appear star-struck.

Don't go off the deep-end. Don't start screaming hysterically and pointing at them either while stomping one foot in convulsions.

It's one thing to be genuinely respectful of a brilliant actor/ director/ producer/ writer's work. It's quite another to be a fawning fool.

Big celebrities are bombarded with star-struck fans, so be different, be real.

Even better, ignore them. Mr. Movie Star is not used to being ignored, and he might come up to talk to you. Try it, and you will see.

It works.

Lastly, don't be surprised when you meet Mr. Movie Star, who plays a badass on the silver screen, only to discover that without a script, props and special effects, in real life he is a wimp and has nothing to say.

Lesson #36: It's a Wrap

Now that you've learned some life-saving tips on how to survive and get ahead in the mud pit that is Los Angeles let's wrap it up.

There are few do-overs in Hollywood.

As you now know wanting to make it big in the entertainment industry can be dangerous business.

Despite all of this don't become jaded or discouraged. There are still some good guys out there. Thank God not all men are twisted dirtbags—just like not all women are slutty tramps or bimbos.

While this book may be broad-stroked as a man-bash book, au contraire, it is a *dirtbag bash book*. That's entirely different and fair game.

Let's hear it for the good guys out there. Applause! Applause! You get a standing ovation.

If you are not a powerful or famous sleazeball, this book should not have bothered you one bit.

So now, I ask you. Where is everyone who was once full of promise with high-flying stardom dreams?

Some people got out in one piece.

A few got lucky.

A number of them caught their 15-minutes of fame, and then ended up in the dustbin of Hollywood history, a butt of late-night comedian jokes. Others are dead.

Where are you today? Which direction are you going to take?

Whenever you get frustrated or jealous when you think you see other people soaring above you, take a deep breath.

Look through the smoke and mirrors and the manufactured façade that is Hollywood that you have just learned about. Now you know how to view the real picture.

Coveting is for losers. Especially when you know the price some people have paid for fame and fortune.

Ask yourself during those sell-out moments of temptation that you will face if it will be worth a lifetime of losing your soul over.

As you chase the brass ring, will you compromise yourself for stuff and false idol worship that you can't take with you when you die?

Are you going to be caught with your pants down?

There are no overnight successes. Behind every overnight success are years of hardship and struggle. Nothing comes easy.

Be patient. Keep working hard.

Your time will come.

Good girls have longevity and will be employable when they are forty +. They will have skills, the body of work based on talent and their self-respect.

You can't put a price tag on self-respect. Anything a good girl has earned will be based on hard work, perseverance and not because she gave the best blow jobs ever.

Slutty tramps, Barbie-doll bimbos and good-time girls, will have a tough time in the long run, assuming they are still walking among us. What are they going to do when nobody wants their legs open anymore?

The bloom on every rose fades. Watching a former drop-dead, gorgeous, aspiring actress panic as she ages and bee-lines it to the plastic surgeon's office is not a pretty sight.

Respect yourself, honey, because in this town, no one else will.

You see? You can get ahead and catch breaks while keeping your legs closed.

Welcome to Hollywood. Good luck!

About the Author

R.W. MILLS is a former Hollywood insider. Currently Mills is considering expanding some of the lessons into their own books.

i Alison Boshoff, "In one face, the real price of fame: As Melanie Griffith is pictured looking eerily smooth-skinned at 56, how her face charts the highs and lows of a troubled life," *Daily Mail Online*, October 31, 2013. Access online: http://www.dailymail.co.uk/femail/article-

2482446/Melanie-Griffiths-face-charts-highs-lows-troubled-life.html
Also see Jessica Simpson here:
http://celebrilarity.com/2008/05/04/jessica-simpson-no-more-duck-lips-again.html
ii Fact and Statistics About Drug and Alcohol Abuse, *American Psychological Association for Los Angeles County*. September 2014.
Access online:
http://losangeles.networkofcare.org/mh/library/article.aspx?id=393

iii Monique Roffey, "Health: When masturbation can be fatal: The practice of auto-erotic asphyxia is often concealed by a coroner's verdict."
The Independent, September 9, 2014. Access online:
http://www.independent.co.uk/life-style/health-and-families/health-news/health-when-masturbation-can-be-fatal-the-practice-of-autoerotic-asphyxia-is-often-concealed-by-a-coroners-verdict-monique-roffey-looks-at-a-lethal-taboo-1484619.html

iv Brian Alexander, "Actor's death raises bizarre questions," *MSNBC*, June 5, 2009. Access online:
http://www.nbcnews.com/id/31129156/ns/health-sexual_health/t/actors-death-raises-bizarre-questions/#.VANYqssg__8

v Thomas R. King and John Lippman, "*Fatal Attraction:* How Sex and Drugs Brutally Ripped Apart Hot Hollywood Team," *Wall Street Journal*, January 26, 1996. Access online:
http://online.wsj.com/public/resources/documents/king1-26-96.htm
vi John M. Glionna, Beverly Hills Madam Elizabeth Adams Dies, *Los Angeles Times*, July 11, 1995. Access online:
http://articles.latimes.com/1995-07-11/local/me-22546_1_beverly-hills-madam
vii Hugo Martin, "Death of a Salesman: Party animal Charlie Minor was a star in the shadowy world of record promotion, pushing many artists to the top. He was shot to death in March, just as he was trying to slow his hectic lifestyle." Los Angeles Times, September 24, 1995. Access online:
http://articles.latimes.com/1995-09-24/entertainment/ca-49278_1_death-march
viii Fluffer, *Urban Dictionary*. Access online:
http://www.urbandictionary.com/define.php?term=fluffer&page=2
ix Matt Wilstein, "Katie Couric Reportedly Wondered Who Diane Sawyer 'Blew this time" to Land Exclusive Interview,'" Mediaite, August 27, 2014. Access online: http://www.mediaite.com/online/katie-couric-reportedly-wondered-who-diane-sawyer-blew-this-time-to-land-exclusive-interview/
x Frank Swertlow, "Anthony Pellicano Denied Bail After Impassioned Anita Busch Plea," *The Wrap*, August 13, 2012. Access online:
http://www.thewrap.com/movies/article/anthony-pellicano-denied-

R.W. MILLS

bail-after-impassioned-anita-busch-plea-51771/